The
Hunted

The Crystal Coast Series

The Hunted

Chrissy Lessey

Tenacious Books Publishing

Published in 2017 by Tenacious Books Publishing
tenaciousbooks@gmail.com

Library of Congress Cataloging-in-Publication Data
The Hunted / Chrissy Lessey
ISBN 978-0-9989518-2-9 (e-book)
ISBN 978-0-9989518-3-6 (print)

Cover Image: © iStock
Cover Design: Anita B. Carroll www.race-point.com
Book Design: Erin Rhew www.erinrhewbooks.com

Printed in the United States of America

www.tenaciousbookspublishing.com

For Jacob and Sarah

prologue

December 1691

Lucia braced herself against the bitter wind and stomped toward the home she shared with her mother, Diana. Longing for sunny days and milder weather, she pulled her wool cape tighter around herself and pressed on.

She waved at a passing neighbor. Receiving only a curt nod in return, she pressed her lips together. Life had never been easy here, but there had once been a time when friendly greetings and laughter filled the air. Since Reverend Samuel Parris had taken over the church two years earlier, those moments of simple joy had grown ever fleeting.

She reached the thick wooden door of her home and pushed it open. Her mother stood in the kitchen, adding another log to the fire that blazed in their enormous hearth. A bean pot hung over the flames, greeting Lucia with the comforting scent of molasses, salted pork, and onions. She looked forward to their evening meal, which they would enjoy with a hearty brown bread her mother had made earlier that day.

"Hello, my dear." Diana twirled around to welcome her. "Come, stand by the fire and rid yourself of that chill."

Lucia kept her cape and bonnet on as she poised her hands over the flames. "I think it will snow tonight." She shivered. The fire did little to ease the cold that coursed through her. She rubbed her palms together in a futile attempt to warm herself and stepped away from the hearth.

"I believe you're right. Seems we are in for a long winter." Diana lifted the cover on the bean pot and added fresh water to the aromatic mixture. "John Anderson inquired about you today." She cast a sideways glance at her daughter. "He seemed *very* interested."

Lucia curled her lip in disgust. "He's an old man."

"That he is, and wrinkled as a dried prune too." Diana laughed. "Fortunately for you, he was asking for his son, Andrew. Now, *he* is a handsome fellow." She raised her eyebrows. "What do you think?"

"No." Lucia fiddled with her auburn braid. "They aren't like us, Mother. They have no magic. I don't want to have to keep who I am a secret from my husband." Their neighbors' concept of religious freedom only extended as far as their own Puritan beliefs. Just one slip up could trigger the same catastrophic witch hunts that had chased her people from England. She'd rather live alone than risk that.

"My dear, you have already reached your twenty-third year. Your time to be picky has passed." Diana paused for a moment, and her gaze shifted to the fire. "Our numbers are dwindling. There is only one way to fix that."

Lucia couldn't argue that point. They'd already lost too many of their kind during the hunts in Europe. The time had come to fortify their numbers—or risk extinction. "I will consider it." She sighed, resigned.

She removed her cape and bonnet, hung them on a hook beside the door, and then sat down at their small table.

"Good." Diana patted her daughter's shoulder. "Now tell me, have you had any more visions?"

Lucia groaned and tossed her braid over her shoulder. "Yes, but I can't make any sense of it. The images are jumbled, and I don't see how it could possibly come true."

"This is a new gift. It will take time to master. You have to learn to separate your own thoughts and desires from the visions themselves." She hunched forward as a grin tugged at the corners of her mouth. "Tell me what you saw."

Lucia let her gaze drift to the fire. "It is an island with a sandy shore. Blue ocean water stretches before me, as far as I can see. Soft green grass grows on the land behind the beach, and the sun shines brightly upon it. Every time I see it, I feel happy."

Diana's eyes brightened with delight. "It sounds lovely. Who is with you on this island?"

"I think that's why the vision brings me such happiness, Mother." Lucia tucked a stray hair behind her ear. "I see only our people there. No one else. We do not have to hide our ways."

"Paradise." Diana settled on the stool across from Lucia with a dreamy look in her eyes. "Perhaps that is where we are meant to be."

Someone pounded on the door. Diana rose to her feet right away and pulled it open—sending the flames in the fireplace into wild flickers as a rush of biting winter wind swept through the cottage. After the cold blast struck Lucia, she peered around her mother to see who had arrived.

William Sawyer, one of their neighbors, waited on their doorstep, bouncing from one foot to another in a frantic, anxious dance. In spite of the frigid temperature, beads of sweat had gathered on his forehead. Lucia grinned. She'd seen this same scenario countless times before.

"The baby is coming." Breathless and wide-eyed, their neighbor rambled with excited urgency. "Can you help her?"

Diana snatched her cloak from the hook beside the door and draped it over her shoulders. "Yes, of course." She gave Lucia a wink. "I will be at the Sawyer's home this evening. Go ahead and eat. Don't wait for me."

Lucia added another log to the fire and stood close to the flames. Resisting the warmth of the blaze, an unshakeable chill had only deepened within her during her mother's lengthy absence. She frowned, unwilling to stand around and allow her fears to besiege her. Perhaps there had been trouble during the birth, and if so, maybe she could help. It beat standing around in the house, wondering and freezing.

She stepped away from the hearth and reached for her cape. Before she had a chance to grab it, the door flew open and Diana rushed in, slamming it behind her.

"Mother, I was getting worried! Did Goody Sawyer have a boy or a girl?" Lucia clasped her hands together and raised them to her chest in excitement.

Diana pressed her lips into a tight line as she removed her cloak. She placed it on the hook and whipped around to face her daughter.

Bold crimson stains stretched across her apron and skirt. With a gasp, Lucia clamped her hand over her mouth.

Diana stared down at the dark smears and then met Lucia's gaze. "I was able to save the baby boy." The creases in her forehead deepened. "But I could not help Goody Sawyer. She is gone."

"I'm so sorry." Lucia knew the depth of her mother's care for her patients. The pain of this loss would stay with her for a very long time.

"Oh, Lucia. I told them to fetch the doctor for me." Diana yanked off her soiled apron with more force than necessary and threw it on the floor. "He might have been able to save her."

"They ignored your request?"

"Yes!" Diana raked her shaky fingers through her graying hair. "They summoned Reverend Parris instead."

Lucia's gaze fell to her feet. The physician was one of their kind. He could have healed Goody Sawyer with a simple touch disguised as examination. "Such a terrible loss."

"I couldn't stay over there any longer. Goody Sawyer's body had not even grown cold, yet Reverend Parris stood by her bed declaring her death to be the work of the devil." Diana's jaw tightened. "He's still over there now filling that poor widower's head with his insane superstitions."

Lucia rubbed her forehead with a trembling hand. The overzealous reverend held far too much power in the pious community. She'd always thought him unkind, but now, she feared that his influence would lead to something far more sinister.

Her mind racing, Lucia prepared a serving of beans and a thick slice of brown bread for her tired mother. She joined Diana at the table, and together, they sat in silence.

From beyond the walls of their small cottage, a distant murmur of voices grew louder. Alarmed, Lucia jumped up from the table and raced to the narrow window beside the door. She spotted the source of the unsettling sounds right way. They were coming. With raised fists, angry chants, and burning torches, they were coming.

"Mother!" She whirled around to face Diana.

Diana rushed to her side, joining her at the window. After just a quick glance, she pushed Lucia away and secured the door with a heavy board.

"It's happening again, isn't it?" Lucia's lip quivered as she watched the color drain from her mother's face. "This is just like the witch hunts in England. This is how you described them." *Angry mobs and executions.* Her breath caught in her throat.

Diana nodded. The voices outside grew even louder, and their enraged shouts became clearer.

"The midwife is a witch!"

"She killed Goody Sawyer!"

Diana pressed her back against the door, as if her presence could somehow stop the mob from breaking through. Her chest heaved with rapid, desperate breaths. "Come here, daughter."

Without a word, Lucia obeyed her mother and stood before her. Icy tendrils of dread coursed through her body, forcing a new shiver to race up her spine. A flicker of light flashed in the narrow window, growing brighter as the fire from the mob's torches drew closer. Her heart thundered in her chest. They were out of time.

Diana grabbed Lucia's hands and gazed into her eyes. "You must gather the others right away. Our boats are still in the harbor. Go tonight and find your island. Be the queen our people need."

"What? Mother, no!" Overwrought, Lucia shook her head in adamant refusal. "I will stay with you!"

"There has already been enough death tonight. I cannot let you become a part of it." She paused, studying Lucia's face as if to save the memory of her image forever. "Remember all that I taught you. Teach the same to your children when they come. Do this for me." She wrapped her arms around her daughter in a final embrace.

Tears flowed unabated down Lucia's cheeks. She clung to her mother, unwilling to let go and follow the command she'd been given.

Lucia noticed Diana's breath slow. She knew her mother had made up her mind, resigned to an unthinkable fate.

Diana pulled away and placed her hand below her neck, bringing her hidden amethyst pendant into view. She reached for its thick gold chain and pulled it over her head.

"This is your legacy." She slipped the necklace around Lucia's neck. The door rattled behind them as the mob pounded against it, but Diana ignored them and straightened the pendant. "Hide it."

Lucia cupped the amethyst and focused her energy until the necklace vanished.

Furious voices demanded that Diana emerge from the house and answer for the sin she had not committed.

"You know what will happen now. You know what you must do." She stroked Lucia's cheek. "What a wonderful queen you will be."

The amethyst weighed heavy on Lucia's chest. Even as her heart shattered, she nodded, acknowledging her duty. She had trained for such an event since she was a little girl. Still, nothing could have prepared her for the pain of this moment.

With a gentle nudge, Diana pushed Lucia away from the door. She took in a deep breath, squared her shoulders, and held her head high. With one final, wistful glance at Lucia, she lifted the heavy board that had kept the door secure.

The mob swarmed through the threshold like cockroaches. William Sawyer led the charge, anger and grief evident on his red, tear-streaked face. Reverend Parris strode in behind him and pointed an accusing finger at Diana. A dozen more friends and neighbors surged forward, crowding the tiny cottage, their features distorted with rage and contempt. Many more waited outside, shouting slurs and waving torches.

"There she is." Reverend Parris jabbed his finger toward Diana. "That's the midwife!"

Lucia lurched forward, blocking the angry men from reaching her mother. "No!" There had to be a way to stop them without revealing her power. She blinked back hot tears.

"Move away, girl!" The reverend sneered. "Unless you want to share your mother's punishment."

Diana's whisper came from behind her, soft but unflinching. "It is my time, daughter. Not yours."

One man stepped forward and cocked his head toward Lucia. "She has not been accused of a crime."

The reverend narrowed his eyes narrowed as he scowled at her. "Not yet."

Lucia glared at him for a long moment, knowing a misstep now could result in her arrest as well. She drew in a ragged breath, unwilling to leave her mother unprotected.

"I am ready." Diana leaned in close to Lucia's ear. "And so are you."

Reverend Parris nodded to one of the men in the group, triggering a frenzy of movement inside the cramped cottage. In the chaos, someone shoved Lucia away from her mother. She stumbled backward and slammed into the kitchen table.

Attempting to steady herself, she watched, helpless, as the blacksmith and one of the village carpenters rushed to Diana. They yanked her arms, throwing her off-balance. Lucia grimaced at the unnecessary show of force, knowing her mother would have left with them peacefully if given the opportunity.

As the men dragged Diana across the threshold, she cast a final glance back at her daughter. Determined not to break their connection, Lucia held her mother's gaze until she disappeared into the dark, frigid night.

The mob was gone. Her mother was gone. She buried her face in her hands and listened to the retreating cacophony. In those long, excruciating moments, Lucia never heard a single cry from Diana, only the hysterical ranting and raving of a village gone mad.

Lucia raised her head and wiped her tears away. She'd have to be strong, like her mother. *Somehow.*

Alone, she blinked and glanced about their modest quarters, hollow now without the warmth of Diana's presence. She didn't know how to proceed. Her mother would have known what to do. She'd *always* known what to do. Lucia's stomach clenched at the thought of her.

A strange heat began to emanate from the amethyst in spite of the disguising spell she had placed on it. She remained still for a moment, waiting for the amulet to reveal its secrets.

Then it came. A flurry of unexpected memories. Memories that were not her own. One by one, episodes from thousands of years of triumph and hardship flashed through her mind. First, she witnessed a time when all of humanity respected her kind, a stark contrast to her experience in Salem Village.

The memories came faster. Babies born, spells cast, and wars waged. Then, something changed. The very people who had once loved the witches turned against them. Kings and queens no longer sought the sorceress' counsel. Instead, those same leaders began to hunt the witches.

Fires and nooses. Pain and anguish. The memories flooded through her. Oh, how her people had suffered! Lucia squeezed her eyes shut as wave after wave of emotion hit her. Over the centuries, her people had run from land to land seeking the peaceful life they so desperately craved. She felt every bit of it, all of the loss, all of the heartbreak. It was hers and hers alone to endure. She gripped the edge of the table, bracing herself for more images of hate, ignorance, and rabid superstition.

As the final unfamiliar memories streamed through her mind, Lucia came to understand the full scope of her responsibility. It was bigger than her, bigger than this village, bigger even than rescuing her mother from certain death. Drawing from a genetic depth of potent will, just as her mother had done only moments before, Lucia squared her shoulders and held her head high. She drew in a deep breath as she wiped away her tears. With a final glance around her home, she marched through the threshold one last time.

She would gather her people and find the island paradise of her vision.

Lucia would be the queen they needed.

Chapter One

Stevie

Present Day

S tevie and Dylan strolled along the shore in companion-able silence. Waves pounded against the sand, propelling a rush of water toward their bare feet with each crash. Though it was as hot as any summer day, only a few sunbathers dotted the beach on this Sunday morning.

She inhaled a great breath of salty air. At the height of vacation season, the scent of chemical sunscreen permeated the air along the shore. Now that the tourists were gone, the blissful, pure fragrance of the ocean reigned supreme once again. Wispy white clouds danced across the pale blue backdrop of the heavens, as if they too relished the beauty of the day.

With all of the unexpected twists and turns her life had taken, Stevie found peace in the constant crash of the waves and the cool sensation of the sea breeze on her skin. She closed her eyes, recalling the words Dylan had whispered just before her mother inducted her into the coven. *Tonight, Stevie, everything is going to change.*

Indeed, everything had changed that night when her dormant magical abilities surfaced. Many of the people she'd known her entire life turned out to be genetic witches, her own mother their queen. To top it all off, Charlie's powers had manifested as well—presenting a whole new set of challenges for her autistic son. She opened her eyes and blinked at the brightness of the sun's rays.

When it all began, Stevie had been so desperate to keep Charlie safe from the danger presented by Vanessa Moore, she hadn't considered the logistics of her new circumstances. Now, she understood the gift of her powerful magic came with a lifetime of secrets to protect at all costs.

Everything is *different now.*

She let the beach work its own magic on her worries, sighing as warm water washed over her toes. The combination of salty breeze and the whoosh of crashing waves soothed her fears, if only for a moment. Her senses had sharpened with the onset of her magical abilities, and she reveled in the enhanced experience of a simple walk on the beach. A seagull cried overhead as it swooped in to grab an abandoned sandwich crust. Stevie smiled. The ocean provided her with a constant—always churning, always perfect.

Dylan broke their comfortable silence. "Are you sending Charlie back to school tomorrow? He's done really well this week."

"That's the plan." Stevie tightened her ponytail and avoided his gaze.

He cocked his head. "You sound uncertain."

"Well, he hasn't had any slip ups, but there's so much riding on his ability to keep his magic hidden. It's crucial that we keep our heritage a secret, and I'm not sure he understands how important it is." She let her gaze drift over the ocean. "He has to go back soon though. He's already missed too much school."

She had yet to come up with a good explanation for Charlie's extended absence from class. While his kindergarten teacher practiced solitary witchcraft and understood the choice to keep Charlie home, Stevie still had to write a fictional note explaining her son's absence to satisfy the school system's attendance requirements.

Stevie pursed her lips. Secrets and lies. She hated both of them.

"Charlie can do this, Stevie. It'll be okay." Dylan rubbed her back as they continued their walk.

"But he's so young. He could make a mistake. What if he used magic while he was with his dad this weekend?" She threw her arms up. "How am I going to explain that?"

Dylan reached for her hand and gave it a gentle squeeze.

She stopped walking and pivoted to face him. "And school! There are so many things that could go wrong there. What if he turns off the electricity in the building? You know how he hates those fluorescent lights. Or, what if a kid is mean to him, and Charlie decides to turn him into a frog? He's extremely powerful. Anything could happen." She shook her head. "The possibilities are endless."

Dylan tugged Stevie's hand, pulling her closer. "Charlie's not the first one of us to develop powers at a young age, you know. Our people have been in Beaufort for centuries, and the secret has never been revealed." He lifted her chin until she met his steady gaze. "But I know better than to tell you not to worry, so I'll just have to distract you instead."

He bent down until his lips met hers, and for a euphoric moment, Stevie's worries slipped away. She wrapped her arms around his waist and rested her head on his broad chest.

Her smile returned. "Mission accomplished."

"Good." Dylan kissed her forehead. He took her hand again, and they resumed their easy pace along the shore.

As they passed an empty lifeguard stand, Stevie nodded toward it. "I don't think I ever told you, but I was an Atlantic Beach lifeguard the summer after you left for London."

"I bet you were adorable." Dylan gave her a playful wink.

"Oh yeah, that's what lifeguards want to be known for." Stevie swatted his arm. "Actually, the training was pretty intense. We all had to get certified in CPR too."

"Did you have to rescue a lot of swimmers?"

"I only assisted in one rescue. In all honesty, I mostly just sat in the guard stand and blew my whistle…a lot."

"Oh, I see." Dylan gave her a sidelong glance. "Well, in that case, I'm sticking with adorable."

Stevie answered him with another swat and a giggle. "You're terrible."

Dylan checked his watch. "We should probably start heading back now." He turned around toward the parking lot.

"Yeah, I want to get home before Sam arrives with Charlie."

"Have you told Sam about us yet?" He kept walking, his gaze fixed on the long stretch of sand ahead of them.

Stevie stole a glimpse of his face. The playfulness, present just a moment before, had disappeared. She cleared her throat. "Not yet. There just hasn't been a good time for that discussion."

Dylan nodded. "Don't rush on my account." His forced smile did little to mask the disappointment in his deep, brown eyes.

"It's the right thing to do. He needs to know." She paused. "I'll take care of it today."

Stevie just had to figure out how to tell her ex-husband, who was still in love with her, that she had moved on. She grimaced and kneaded the tight knot that had begun to form on her neck. *But how am I supposed to do that?*

chapter two

Vanessa

Vanessa sipped from her juice box as she glanced around her small hospital room. There were no cards or flowers from concerned friends and family members. Instead, images of garish, anthropomorphic animals and gaudy balloons adorned each wall. She sighed and pressed the button on her morphine pump while an obese teddy bear gawked at her from its seat in the corner.

She drained her juice and returned it to the tray table. She'd volunteered to pay out-of-pocket for the luxury of a private room when she was released from Intensive Care, and the administration of the community hospital had been happy to oblige. With the adult wards filled to capacity with flu patients, they'd transferred her to a room on the pediatric floor instead. For two long weeks, she'd endured nauseating wall art, condescending nurses, and juice. So much juice.

And then there was the doctor, who poked and prodded her on a daily basis. While he'd worked, he'd explained that her injuries included a concussion, two cracked ribs, and a combination of second and third-degree burns along the left side of her body, as well as on her face and scalp. More than once he'd reminded her that he had seen worse injuries. He'd even suggested that she was very fortunate to have survived such an ordeal, as if remaining alive were some sort of prize.

It wasn't. She clenched her fist, resisting the overwhelming urge to scratch one of her healing burns.

He, along with other hospital staff, had asked numerous times about the cause of her injuries. Each time she'd answered, "I don't remember."

But she did remember. She remembered all of it. It haunted her in jumbled flashes of memory—the explosion of the boat, the acrid scent of her hair burning, the confusion. Then the pain, the unimaginable pain.

She grimaced, recalling the details of the night that had changed the trajectory of her life. She'd shot Dylan and fought with Stevie. Sticking to her plan, she'd even gone after the boy as well. Vanessa had expected Stevie to be protective of him. She'd counted on it, in fact—figuring the devoted mother would divulge the location of the amulet if her child's life depended on it. But nothing could have prepared her for Stevie's ferocity in defending him. Vanessa certainly had not anticipated that the new witch would attack while she made her escape.

Despite her best efforts to please her insane mother, Vanessa still had not been able to find the magical amulet. And she'd lost everything in the process. She let her gaze drift to the window, glimpsing a world that moved on without her.

A knock rattled the door. Without waiting for an answer, a nurse swung it open and entered the room. *Here comes another one.* She stifled an annoyed groan. Staff members barged in and out throughout the day and night. They came to check her wounds and her vitals. They delivered medications and food. Some stopped in to suggest she get out of bed and move around more; others disturbed her just to remind her to get some rest.

With the exception of the fat stuffed bear, she didn't have to share her room with anyone else. But it hardly gave her the privacy she sought.

"Good afternoon, Miss Moore." The nurse wheeled in a vital signs monitor.

As usual, the young woman wore neon pink plastic shoes and well-worn scrubs decorated with pictures of playful kittens. Vanessa hadn't bothered to learn her name, or anyone else's, during her hospital stay. Instead, she'd given them all nicknames. Kitten Pants worked on the weekends while Glitter Shoes cared for her during the week. Ice Hands and Lipstick covered night duty. She detested them all, but Ice Hands was, by far, her least favorite.

She saw no point in asking this one's name now. The shift change would be coming up soon, and another perky, ridiculously dressed pediatric nurse would take her place. Vanessa ignored her as she approached the bedside.

Kitten Pants glanced at the IV pump. "You're up to your limit on the morphine again."

"Still hurts." Vanessa did not meet her gaze.

"Aww." She cocked her head and offered a melodramatic pout. "What hurts?"

My heart, my pride, my soul.

"My burns, my head, my ribs." Vanessa rolled her head against her pillow, its plastic cover crackled in protest against her movement.

"I'll let your doctor know." She clipped a sensor to the tip of Vanessa's right index finger and slipped a digital thermometer under her tongue. Humming while she worked, the nurse wrapped a blood pressure cuff around the unburned arm and pushed a button.

Vanessa winced as the cuff tightened on her arm and listened for the series of electronic dings that would signal the end of this twice-daily injustice. At long last, the beeps rang out, and Kitten Pants removed the thermometer, cuff, and sensor.

The nurse tossed the gadgets into the basket under the vital signs monitor. "Everything's normal."

Vanessa stifled a groan. Nothing about this was *normal*.

"Now, let's see how your burns are healing." She moved around to Vanessa's left side.

First, Kitten Pants checked the minor leg burns. Then, she shifted her attention to the more serious wounds on Vanessa's left arm. With great care, she began to unwrap the gauze bandages.

Vanessa glanced down at the crimson blotches covering the length of her arm and bit her lip. Most of the damage had been second-degree, though there were several scattered spots of deeper burns. They had finally begun to heal, but that knowledge brought her little comfort. The scars were as gruesome as her seared flesh.

Her face hurt the most. She clenched her teeth in anticipation of the next round of bandage removal. She had not yet glimpsed at herself in a mirror—not without the bandages anyway—but she remained constantly aware of the area of raw tissue across her left cheek, which extended to her scalp.

Much of her long, black mane had burned in the explosion, leaving choppy patches of singed, short hair surrounding the bald, scorched area of her scalp. A few long locks remained on the right side of her head. She stroked one of the sparse tendrils that cascaded down the front of her hospital gown, a cruel reminder of the beautiful woman she had once been. Vanessa knew she should just cut them off, but that would require more time in front of a mirror. She wasn't ready for that yet.

"No sign of infection." Kitten Pants began to apply fresh bandages. "Your leg and arm are healing nicely, but there are a couple of places on your face and scalp that still have a long way to go."

"How bad do you think the scarring will be?" She'd asked the same question during previous examinations, each time hoping for better news that never came. She swallowed hard, envisioning a lonely, miserable future. It was a life that wasn't even worth living.

"You'll have to talk to the doctor about that." The nurse placed a fresh bandage on Vanessa's cheek, her expression grim.

These scars will stay with me forever. Vanessa squeezed her eyes closed for a long moment.

The doctor had told her most of the burns would heal without significant intervention, rendering a transfer to the burn unit in Chapel Hill unnecessary. If everything went well, it was unlikely that she would need any skin grafts. He had explained this while ardently reminding her how very lucky she was.

She would have been lucky if she'd stayed in Los Angeles and never returned to North Carolina at all. In addition to failing in her quest to retrieve the amulet, she'd lost her magic abilities courtesy of the Beaufort coven. Now she had a lifetime of burn scars to look forward to as well. She was powerless and hideous, exactly the opposite of what she'd been before returning to the Crystal Coast. Fortune hadn't been on her side at any point in this endeavor. It sure as hell wasn't with her now.

26

Vanessa had only wanted to please her mother, and that desire had almost killed her. Did Susan even know about the explosion? Probably not. *I'll bet she noticed I didn't come back with the amulet.*

She'd considered calling Susan several times since her arrival at the hospital. As much as she craved comfort from her mother, Vanessa suspected she would receive only more criticism. But she'd have to do it soon. The longer she put it off, the angrier Susan would be when they finally spoke.

"Do you need anything before I go?" The nurse stepped toward the door.

"No." Vanessa turned back toward the window.

Chapter three

Susan

Slouched in a vinyl chair next to the day room window, Susan watched a black bird fly around the old oak tree in the courtyard. She coveted the bird's freedom. It could go anywhere and do whatever it pleased. All she had to look forward to was the next dose of mind-numbing pharmaceuticals prescribed by her psychiatrist. Though she hated him for keeping her trapped in such a miserable place, she had to admit she appreciated his liberal use of the prescription pad.

The medicinal comfort kept her calm in spite of all that had gone wrong with her escape plan. With Vanessa missing, she could only assume that her daughter had failed in her mission. Again. She shook her head. It had been foolish to expect anything else from her worthless child. Almost as foolish as it had been to hope for anything beyond the punishment she now endured.

Susan had been powerful once. Powerful enough to flick a car from a bridge with little more than a thought. She closed her eyes, savoring the memory. She'd give anything to have it all back.

With a heavy sigh, she glanced across the expanse of the day room. A few patients passed their time either watching television or putting together tattered puzzles with missing pieces. Calm and compliant, they all appeared content with their lot in life. But then again, they belonged here. She did not.

The wall-mounted clock, which hung over the old television set, marked the passing of another hour with a click. Her morning medication was long overdue. She jerked her head toward the doorway in search of a nurse.

Susan tapped her fingers on the arm of the chair as agitation bubbled within her. She needed her chemical serenity now more than ever. She didn't want to feel *anything*.

Her shifting gaze settled on the hospital chaplain, who sat alone at a table scribbling notes on a yellow legal pad. He came by every Sunday morning to lead a worship service for the patients and staff. He often met with patients afterward for individual counseling and prayer, two services that Susan had no intention of ever utilizing. Her soul was beyond saving.

She studied the chaplain through narrowed eyes, thinking he looked like a mouse of a man. Small-framed and timid, with an unshakeable grin, he was hardly menacing. And yet, she felt an intense discomfort every time she saw him. She stifled a shudder. No matter the century or the circumstances, nothing good happened when their kinds crossed paths.

"Susan?" A nurse called to her from the doorway.

You'd better have my damn medicine ready. She whipped her head toward the nurse, ready to snap about her failure to perform her duties. Taking in the young woman's wide-eyed expression, curiosity quelled her rage. "What is it?"

"There's a phone call for you. You can take it at the nurse's station."

Susan had never received a call during her lengthy hospitalization. Puzzled, she rose and made her way across the room.

Together, they crossed the hallway to the station, where another nurse held a corded telephone receiver. She raised her eyebrows in curiosity as she passed the receiver to Susan. Neither nurse made any effort to disguise their interest. Instead, they both stared at her as she jerked the phone toward her chest.

"Do you mind?" Susan waved them away like flies.

With a start, both women busied themselves at the station but remained well within earshot. One shuffled papers around. The other developed a sudden interest in organizing the contents of the paperclip dispenser.

With an exasperated sigh, Susan pressed the phone to her ear. "Who is this?"

"It's Vanessa." The familiar voice came through, raspy and weak. "Mother, I—"

Susan set her jaw. "Did you get it?" She glared at the nurses, who'd stopped to watch her again. They resumed their tasks with renewed commitment, each competing to be more engrossed in mediocrity than the other.

"Mother, I've been hurt…there was an explosion."

"Answer me!" She balled her hand into a tight fist. "Did you get it?"

"I…I tried to, on the night of the hurricane. But Stevie blew up the boat I was on." Vanessa paused. "I have terrible burns, broken ribs, and a concussion. I'm in the hospital now."

"So you're saying you failed." Susan pounded her fist against the desk. "Again."

"I'm sorry, Mother." Vanessa spoke in barely more than a whisper.

Susan's hands trembled in the wake of her own fury. She hadn't been this angry in years. With the nurses and orderlies waiting nearby, she couldn't do damned thing about it.

She tightened her grip on the receiver while a litany of her daughter's numerous failings raced through her addled mind. She wanted to lash out, but she bit her tongue. Instead, she threw the phone down on the desk so hard it bounced back up before coming to a rest.

"Hang it up." She stomped back toward the day room. "I have nothing more to say to her."

Chapter four

Stevie

Stevie paced across her kitchen floor while she waited for Sam to return with Charlie. She chewed her lip, considering all the things she'd kept from her ex-husband. She'd have to tell him about her relationship with Dylan. That much she knew. But, more than anything, she wanted to tell him that Charlie had spoken.

Charlie's first word in three years had been "magic." That utterance had been a pivotal event in his life, but she'd kept it a secret because Sam would want to know what had led up to the momentous occasion. A knot of guilt twisted in her stomach. That was something Stevie could never reveal. Though it was just one of the many secrets she now kept, it was the one that hurt her soul the most.

She reached the laundry room door, spun around, and paced back toward the refrigerator. Charlie had said "magic" on two other occasions when they'd been alone together. Both times, he'd said it after she'd used her magical gifts. Since he was using his new word appropriately, the odds of Sam hearing it were low.

Words. Of all of the symptoms of Charlie's autism, his lack of communication skills was the most profound. Now that she knew he was physically able to talk, she wondered how long it would be before he said something else. Then Sam could hear his son's voice for himself. And Stevie would have one less secret to keep.

She shook her head, frustrated by the endless cycle of wonder and worry that plagued her. Sam and Charlie would arrive soon, and she still needed to figure out how she was going to break the news about her relationship with Dylan.

Planning to invite Sam in for what she hoped would be a calm discussion, she poured water into her coffee maker and pressed the power button. As the rich scent of the fresh brew filled the air, she tried to think of what she would say. She crossed her arms and leaned against the counter. It would be best to be direct and leave no room for misunderstanding. She didn't want to hurt him, but this conversation had to happen.

When Stevie heard the unmistakable rumble of Sam's old pickup truck on the street, she made her way to the front door. She paused for a moment as she gripped the doorknob, gathering her courage. She had a promise to keep and a life to live.

Stepping outside onto her porch, she watched Charlie emerge from Sam's truck. He held his tablet close and kept his head down as he followed the concrete path into their small front yard.

"Hi, Charlie!" Stevie strode to the edge of the porch, closing the distance between herself and her son. She spread her arms wide, excited to welcome him home.

Carrying the little boy's backpack, Sam followed Charlie along the walkway to the house. "He had a good weekend. We went out to Shackleford yesterday and saw some of the wild horses. I think he liked that."

Stevie smiled. If the horses were the wildest things Sam had witnessed all weekend, then it was safe to assume that Charlie hadn't had any magical slip ups while he was with his dad.

"That sounds like fun." Stevie gave Charlie a hug as soon as he joined her on the porch. She held him close for a moment and then pulled back, hoping to catch a glimpse of his eyes. But he kept his head down.

Though his response, or lack thereof, was not unusual, Stevie felt the all-too-familiar twinge of pain in her heart. She wanted to connect with him, to gaze into his eyes and see his smile. There was so much she didn't know about her own son, and times like this brought the agony of that void to the surface. She reinforced her smile and patted Charlie on the back. "I missed you."

Sam passed the red backpack to Stevie and looked down at Charlie. "Have a good week. I'll see you on Friday." He ruffled his son's golden locks and turned to walk back to his truck.

"Uh, Sam...wait." She paused as Charlie walked inside the house, closing the door behind him. "Do you have a minute? To talk?"

Sam faced her. "Yeah, I guess. What's up?"

"Why don't you come inside? I have a fresh pot of coffee on."

Sam's eyes narrowed as he studied her face. She had no doubt he'd already guessed that this conversation would not be about the reconciliation he'd asked for.

"Just say what you need to say, Stevie." Sam crossed his arms.

She searched for a simple platitude to take the sting out of her next words and realized there was no way to truly soften the blow. Her mouth went dry, but she pressed on. "I just want-ed you to know that I..." She drew in a deep breath, bracing herself for his quick-tempered response. "I'm in a relationship now."

Sam remained silent for an endless moment.

"It's him, isn't it?" He nodded toward Dylan's house.

"Yes." She reached out to touch his arm.

He took a sharp step back. Without a word, he glared at her and shook his head before turning to walk back to his truck.

Stevie sighed. She hadn't expected this to be easy, but she never could have imagined just how much it would hurt. As Sam's old pickup roared to life, she pressed her hand to her chest, attempting to quell an incurable ache.

She went back into her house and closed the door, pausing in the foyer for a moment to collect her thoughts. In spite of the pain of the moment, she could not deny the sense of relief that washed over her. They'd finalized their divorce months ago, but now their split was complete. This was the first time that she truly felt free.

Free to move forward with Dylan. At the thought of him, and the dream of their future together, her stomach fluttered.

Stevie carried Charlie's bag to the kitchen, where she found her son sitting at the table playing a game on his tablet. She placed his backpack on the chair next to him and glanced at her watch. It was time to start cooking their dinner.

"Are you hungry, Charlie?" She expected him to nod. His ability to respond to questions with a nod was another new leap in his development.

Charlie didn't react to her question. Instead, he spun around, reaching for his backpack. He unzipped its front pocket and slipped his hand into the opening.

Stevie tilted her head, watching as he withdrew a pristine, sun-bleached sand dollar.

"Oh, Charlie. It's beautiful." Stevie examined it as he held it out. "I bet we can find a perfect spot in your room to display it."

He pressed the sand dollar toward her.

Stevie gasped. "Is this for me?"

Charlie nodded.

Stevie raised her hand to her mouth. Charlie hadn't given her anything since before his autism diagnosis. Once, as a toddler, he'd plucked a dandelion from their backyard and presented it to her. Her lip quivered at the memory. He'd been so proud of that little yellow weed. It had been a special time, one that she thought she'd never see again. Yet, here they stood more than three years later, and Charlie had presented her with a new treasure.

Overcome with joy, she soon realized there was no stopping the tears that began to pour forth. It was almost too much for her to take. Overwhelmed with love and gratitude, she reached forward to accept this most precious gift from her son.

"Thank you, Charlie." Though she spoke in a whisper, her voice cracked with emotion.

He glanced up, and his eyes met hers for only a second. One perfect second.

All of a sudden, everything changed. Charlie stepped back, his shoulders drawn up tight. Stevie watched the color drain from his face, and she knew in an instant that he'd misunderstood the reason for her tears. She stepped forward to soothe him, but he jerked away. The sand dollar slipped from his hand and crashed onto the tile floor below, shattering into five jagged pieces.

Stevie's heart sank.

Charlie's high-pitched wail rang out, projecting his internal agony throughout the house and straight into Stevie's soul. She stared on, helpless, as he descended into a terrible meltdown.

"No, no, no." She hated herself for crying, for ruining the incredible moment that had been so long coming. She reached out for him once again, wanting only to pull him into her arms.

Charlie backed away until he reached the wall and began to slam his head against it.

"No!" She raced forward and placed her hand between his head and the wall so that she could absorb the impact of the next hit "Don't do that!" She winced as his head bashed her hand into the wall, but she'd rather have her hand smashed to bits than let Charlie hurt himself.

As he lurched forward, preparing to land another strike against the wall, Stevie managed to grab his arms and yank him away. His heartbreaking wail raged on as she sunk down onto the floor behind him. She pressed on the back of his knees, forcing him to sit.

Stevie pulled Charlie onto her lap and wrapped her arms around him. She squeezed him as tight as she could, as if she could hug his autism away. She wanted to explain that her tears had been of joy, not sorrow. She wanted to fix the sand dollar and relive that one perfect moment. But there was no point in voicing her desires. Not yet, anyway. He wouldn't hear her now. Her only option was to let the meltdown run its course and try to keep him safe in the process.

Long, excruciating minutes passed as Stevie held her son. His screams gave way to hoarse whimpers, and Charlie began to rock in her arms. She loosened her grip and rocked back and forth along with him.

Still shaken, she glanced at the clock on her microwave. More than twenty minutes had passed while they sat together on the kitchen floor. Charlie's whimpers soon drifted into the usual silence they were both accustomed to and his rocking slowed to a stop.

In the stillness, Stevie caught her breath. "I love you, Charlie." She kept her voice calm and steady. "Sometimes, people cry from happiness. That's what happened with me. Those tears you saw were not from sadness. I cried because I was so happy you wanted to give me that beautiful sand dollar. Do you understand?"

Stevie remained quiet, giving him the time he needed to process what she had said. After a moment, he nodded.

"Good. Now, I think we can fix the sand dollar with a little magic. Are you ready to try?"

Again, he nodded and then stood up. Stevie rose as well and walked over to the shattered remains of Charlie's gift. Together, they knelt beside it.

"Charlie, put your hands on the sand dollar. Remember what it looked like when you took it out of your backpack." She guided his hand to hover above the broken gift. "Now focus your energy like Grandma showed you and push it into the pieces of the sand dollar."

Stevie beamed with pride as she watched her son concentrate on his magic. "Okay, let's take a peek."

He pulled his hands away to reveal a perfect sand dollar.

Stevie patted his back. "You did it, Charlie!"

He scooped up the treasure and presented it to his mother once again. His gaze flicked up to meet hers, and a hint of a smile danced across his lips. "Magic."

Stevie bit down on her lip, refusing to cry this time. "Thank you." She placed the precious gift on the windowsill above the sink. "Every time I see it, I'll think of you."

Chapter five

Susan

Still fuming from her conversation with Vanessa, Susan stormed into the ward's dayroom. The chaplain glanced up from his yellow notepad and met Susan's glare with a tilt of his head. She averted her gaze, unwilling to share any further interaction with him.

He reached for her but stopped short of laying his hand on her arm. "You seem upset. Would you like to talk about it?"

His northern accent grated on her nerves almost as much as his patronizing smile.

The young minister had tried to connect with her before, to no avail. This time, given her obvious effort to avoid even a shared glance, his boldness only served to enrage her further. She stalked toward his table and clenched her jaw, prepared to tell him exactly what she thought of him *and* his chosen profession.

She glowered at him as she opened her mouth to spew a variety of colorful, hate-filled words, but she stopped herself. Spotting something out of the corner of her eye, she shifted her attention from the chaplain, whose grin had disappeared, and focused on the legal pad resting on the table in front of him. A bold scrawl across the top of the yellow paper formed the words *Malleus Maleficarum*.

"*The Hammer of Witches*." Susan frowned as she uttered the English translation of the old book's title. She took a step back, her body stiff. She stared at the yellow legal pad as if it might leap from the table and bite her.

The chaplain's forehead crinkled in surprise. "You're familiar with the book?"

Susan gave a slow, deep nod. "Very much so." All witches knew of the infamous text that had sparked mass hysteria and brutal witch hunts throughout Europe in the Middle Ages. "It was once the definitive guide to persecuting witches."

The chaplain cleared his throat. "You mean 'prosecuting' witches." He added an arrogant smile for good measure.

"I'm quite sure I know the difference, Chaplain." Disdain gave way to hatred, and Susan sneered at him. She had no patience for this type of lunacy. Why should this chaplain roam freely in the world while she remained captive in a high security psychiatric ward?

She turned her back on him and began to walk away, eager to put as much distance between the two of them as possible. After only a single step, a thought occurred to her. She whirled around to face him once more.

This could not be a coincidence.

Susan stepped forward but hesitated to speak. She knew her shrink would excuse her thoughts as another bout of paranoia. But even in an asylum, an encounter between an overzealous chaplain and a now powerless witch warranted *some* level of suspicion.

She narrowed her eyes and hunched forward. "Why are you here?"

"My family vacationed here when I was a kid." He wrinkled his brow and backed away from her aggressive stance. "I always enjoyed the milder climate. After my parents passed on, I didn't have any reason to stay in Massachusetts. So I decided to move here."

"No." She shook her head at his ridiculous reply. "Why are you *here*? In this hospital?"

"Oh, are you worried that there are witches in the hospital?" The chaplain chuckled. "I can assure you that there aren't any here. Believe me, I would know it."

Susan mimicked his laugh, mocking him. "Why are you interested in that old book anyway?"

The chaplain rested his palm on his notepad, covering the lines of handwritten notes. He studied her face for a moment before he answered. "I guess you could say it's a hobby of mine."

She frowned. There had to be more to the chaplain's fascination with witches than what he'd voiced. She was sure of it. Despite her loathing, she was intrigued by this man who held an interest in a subject that was generally off-limits to those who considered themselves sane. She eased into a chair at the table. "I take it you believe witches are real?"

The chaplain shot a furtive glance around the expanse of the day room. Then, he pushed his legal pad to the side and rested his arms on the table. "Well, they've been around for a very long time. The Bible tells us so, and that's all the proof I need." His hushed tone exuded confidence. "Even for non-believers, it seems that the sheer number of accusers and witnesses throughout history would give even the most ardent skeptic cause for concern."

Susan jerked her chin toward the pad of paper on the table. "What's with the notepad? Are you organizing a witch hunt?" She kept her expression impassive as a new plan formed in her mind.

"Better than that! I'm writing a modernized version of *Malleus Maleficarum*." The chaplain puffed out his chest. "The desire to eliminate witchcraft has fallen out of favor in modern times. I think an updated edition that's relevant to our current circumstances could go a long way toward educating the public on this sinful behavior."

Susan pursed her lips. A book would not serve her plan at all. If she chose her words with care and tiptoed around the constraints of the truth spell inflicted on her by the coven, she might be able to get the pious clod to bend to her will.

She drew in a deep breath. "Perhaps you should consider a witch hunt. I think real world experience would be far more educational than studying the words of long-dead writers."

He sat back in his chair and stroked his chin. "I'm not entirely opposed to the idea, but 'hunt' is a rather strong word. I would, of course, work within the confines of the law. But, yes, I would very much like to locate as many witches as possible."

"And what happens when you find them?" Susan licked her lips. "Will they be burned or hanged?" Either option would suit her just fine.

Regretting her words as soon as she'd uttered them, she stifled a wince. If that stupid nurse had remembered to administer her morning medication, she might not have been so bold as to mention executions. At least not so early in this delicate dance with the devil. It was too late now. She couldn't take back her question. She could only wait for his reaction.

Unfazed by the violent turn in the conversation, the chaplain didn't cringe or pull away. He remained at ease, as if they were planning a church bake sale. "The current laws don't allow for those old style executions." He shrugged. "But we can still call them out for what they are. Public shaming can go a long way toward curbing immorality."

Susan sucked in a slow, deep breath. Did the chaplain speak so openly about his obsession when he was with people who weren't residents of the psychiatric hospital? She guessed not. Otherwise, he'd already be locked in here with her. And then he'd be no use to her at all.

Her mouth curled into the most encouraging smile she could muster. "I can see you've put a lot of thought into this."

"Well, it runs in my family. You see, one of my ancestors was made famous by his quest to bring witches to justice." A proud grin stretched across his thin face. "You've avoided me for so long, perhaps now you'll allow me to introduce myself?"

Susan nodded and narrowed her eyes as she waited for him to continue.

"I am Benjamin Parris, descendant of the great Reverend Samuel Parris. Perhaps you've heard of him?"

Susan sank back against the stiff chair, her heart racing. Of course she'd heard of Samuel Parris. He'd been behind the Salem witch trials in 1692. She stared into the beady eyes of the chaplain in utter disbelief.

She swallowed hard, realizing the opportunity that had fallen into her lap. It was so perfect; for a moment she wondered if she were dreaming. Breathless, she leaned in closer. "I happen to know where you can find some witches."

The chaplain's eyes grew wide. Though his mouth fell open, he did not speak. After a long stretch of silence, he frowned. "Are you mocking me?"

"I assure you, I am not." Susan shook her head. "I have been the victim of magical acts myself. As a matter of fact, that's how I became a prisoner here."

He studied her face, his brow furrowed. "Tell me more."

In the company of anyone else, Susan knew that her status as a mental patient would undermine the seriousness of her claims. But not Chaplain Parris. He would understand the cruelty she'd endured at the hands of the coven because his obsession lent credence to her story.

"There are literally hundreds of witches living in Beaufort." She extended her arms as if to illustrate the full scope of the infestation. "It's shocking really. No one even knows they are there because they've mastered the ability to keep their magic a secret." She rested her palms on the table and lowered her voice even more. "Can you imagine what would happen if word got out?"

The chaplain nodded. "Can you give me the names of all of these witches?" The creases on his forehead flattened and his irksome grin returned. "I would like to…observe them."

"There are just so many, I couldn't begin to list them all. But I can tell you who is in charge." For once, Susan was happy to tell the truth. She pressed her lips together to hide the smile that threatened to betray her.

"I'm listening." Chaplain Parris locked his eyes on hers.

"The ones you should be most concerned with are the members of the coven—the ruling class of witches. They are each quite powerful individually. But they work together, making them nearly unstoppable." *But a good, old-fashioned witch hunt could bring them to their knees in a heartbeat.*

"How would I find this coven?"

"Patricia Guthrie is their leader. In fact, her devotees often refer to her as 'queen.' She claims it's her responsibility to keep all of the other witches safe from people like——" Susan paused for effect.

Chaplain Parris cocked his head. "What people?" He straightened and pointed his thumb toward his chest. "People like me, right?"

"Yes." Susan glanced down and traced her finger along the surface of the table. "You should also know that there's a power amplifying amulet. I believe Patricia is in possession of it. If you can take it from her and bring it to me…" Susan's heart fluttered with excitement as she considered the phrasing of her next statement. "I can end her reign as queen. The others will be easy to flush out once she's out of the way."

The chaplain stared at Susan for a long minute before he nodded. "I'll look into it."

Chapter Six

Stevie

On Monday morning, Stevie dropped Charlie off at school and returned to her home on Front Street. As she emerged from her car, she spotted Dylan standing on his front porch, talking on his phone. She smiled and waved.

He waved back but did not return her smile. She watched him for a moment, noticing his frown and stiff shoulders as he listened to the voice on the other end of the call. He ran his hand through his thick, brown hair and began to speak. Stevie couldn't hear what he was saying, but she knew that he was worried about something.

Instead of interrupting what must be an important call, she stepped inside her house and realized that she still had to tidy up before the day's scheduled coven meeting. Since she'd learned to use her magical gifts, housekeeping was no longer the dreaded task it had once been. She stepped into her living room and found a few of Charlie's toy cars on the floor. With a flick of her wrist, they all popped up from the area rug and flew into a basket, which was nestled in the far corner of the room. The throw pillows promptly fluffed themselves and returned to their usual places on the sofa. She checked the other rooms downstairs, straightening as needed, and then made her way to the kitchen.

"Stevie?" Dylan called from the foyer.

"Come on in. I'm in the kitchen."

She poured two cups of coffee and turned to greet Dylan. "Good morning." Pushing up on her toes, she planted a kiss on his lips.

"Good morning, beautiful." He picked up one of the coffee mugs from the counter. "How did everything go with Charlie's return to school?"

Stevie smiled. She loved that Dylan was interested in her son. "So far, so good. I probably reminded him twenty times this morning that he can't use his magic at school."

Dylan chuckled. "I'm sure you did." His smile faded as he took her hand in his. "I've had a situation come up with one of my charities, and I need to tend to it. I have to fly out right away."

"Is that why you looked so worried outside on the phone?" Stevie squeezed his hand. "Do you really have to go?"

"Yes and yes." He gave two curt nods. "I have to take care of this one personally. There have been allegations that the director of my school in South Africa is embezzling funds. Who else can determine his guilt or innocence faster than I can? It's important that I get the situation under control as quickly as possible."

"Of course. I understand." Stevie sipped her coffee. "How long will you be gone?"

"It's difficult to say for sure. I would guess a week or so, depending on how things go. It could be longer if I have to hire a new director." He shrugged. "Cell service is notoriously unreliable at the school, and the Wi-Fi is spotty on a good day. But I promise I'll call when I can."

Stevie sighed and rested her head on his chest. "I'll miss you."

Shortly before eleven o'clock, the coven members began to arrive at Stevie's house for their scheduled meeting.

Patricia arrived first and greeted her daughter with a warm hug. "Good morning, my dear. We don't have much on the agenda for today's meeting, so it shouldn't take long."

Stevie pulled back and glimpsed the dark bags beneath Patricia's eyes. "Mom, are you okay? You don't look well."

Patricia waved her hand, dismissing the concern. "I'm just a little tired today. Nothing to worry about." She smiled and patted Stevie's arm. "I want you to pay close attention in our meetings. One day, you'll be in charge of the Historic Society and, of course, our coven. You need to learn how we do things."

Stevie groaned. Since her powers manifested weeks earlier, she'd avoided thinking about the leadership role that she would one day inherit. The idea of taking over her mother's responsibilities, both public and secret, overwhelmed her. The women of her family had hidden the activities of the coven under the guise of the Beaufort Historic Society for generations. But all of those women, the queens of the past, had developed their powers much earlier than she had. They'd all had a lifetime of training before they had to fulfill their royal legacies. As a late bloomer, Stevie had serious doubts that she would ever be fit for the job.

"Do we have to keep the two combined? Wouldn't it be easier to separate the Historic Society from the coven?" Stevie had enough on her plate worrying about taking on the responsibility of becoming queen one day. Couldn't the burden of planning fundraisers and festivals for the Historic Society go to someone else?

"I understand your concerns. Really, I do." Patricia squeezed her shoulder. "But without the cover of the Historic Society, people may grow suspicious of our meetings. Throughout time and across continents, that sort of suspicion helped fuel witch hunt madness."

"Yeah, but that was hundreds of years ago! Nothing like that would happen today. Certainly not here."

"I'm sure our ancestors said the same thing before it happened to them. It's simply not worth the risk." She took Stevie's hand in hers. "My daughter, one day you will assume this responsibility just as I did. The coven members will bow down before you, and in that moment, you will fully understand your role in protecting them."

Stevie's eyes grew wide. She couldn't imagine the powerful members of their coven bowing down to anyone, much less her.

The front door swung open, and Stevie heard Lexi's familiar call of "knock, knock" as she let herself in. Deborah, Lexi's mother, followed close behind, carrying her canvas bag full of knitting supplies. They joined Patricia in the living room. Ruth and Randy arrived together soon after, each taking a seat on the sofa. When Ruth scooted herself closer to Randy, Lexi shot a knowing glance at Stevie, who stifled a giggle in return.

"What's so funny?" The numerous lines surrounding Ruth's thin lips grew deeper as she locked eyes with Stevie. She gripped Randy's hand and scowled at the two younger witches. Next to her, the retired doctor grinned.

Stevie blushed. "I'm sorry. It's just...well, I didn't know you two were a couple." She recalled seeing Deborah knit a row of red into her seemingly endless blanket and immediately understood *how* the two of them had come together.

"I think it's fantastic!" Lexi clapped, unfazed by Ruth's sour demeanor. "You two have known each other for decades. How wonderful that you would suddenly—"

"Yes. Yes. It's a wonderful thing, isn't it?" Deborah glanced at her watch. "Look at that! We're already two minutes behind schedule, Patricia. Shouldn't we get the meeting started?"

"There's really not much discuss today. We can take our time." Patricia grinned at her best friend. "Besides, we're still waiting for Alice to get here."

Ruth narrowed her eyes and glared at Deborah. "Why do you look so nervous? Are you responsible for this?" She wagged her finger between herself and Randy.

Deborah cleared her throat. "I may have helped just a bit. But, I didn't interfere with your free will. Clearly, you two were meant to be together. You just needed a little nudge to realize it."

Silence engulfed the room. All eyes turned to Ruth as the coven members awaited a torrent of fury and foul language to erupt from the bitter old woman.

Ruth and Randy shared a glance, and Randy nodded a quiet acknowledgement of some unspoken understanding between them. He leaned forward, meeting Deborah's worried gaze. "We're very happy together." He smiled and lifted Ruth's hand to his lips for a gentle kiss. "I never understood why I had all those visions of Ruth eating dinner alone. But now I know—it's because we were meant to be together. Thank you for giving us the nudge we needed."

Deborah sighed in relief. "You are most welcome."

"In fact, we're leaving this afternoon for a little getaway. We're going to see all of the lighthouses on the Outer Banks." He gave Ruth a sidelong glance. "Isn't that right?"

"Yep." She raised her chin. "It was my idea."

Stevie studied Ruth's thin face. All of her life, this woman had never worn anything but a scowl. Whether in disgust, contempt, anger, or disappointment, Ruth's glower comprised the full range of her emotions. But now, for the first time ever, the slightest hint of a grin graced her lined face, making her look younger than she had in years. Stevie smiled at the thought of the older woman's happiness.

"How romantic!" Deborah patted the bag that held her magical knitting, the same one with a few red rows dedicated to Ruth and Randy. She cast a knowing glance to Patricia.

Patricia gave a wide-eyed shrug but said nothing.

Alice arrived, breathless. "I'm sorry I'm late. I had some things to tend to at church, and they took longer than I expected." She settled into a seat next to Patricia. "Our pastor has come down with the flu, so I had to find someone else to deliver the sermon this Sunday. It's hard to find someone on such short notice, but I did it." She tucked a stray white curl behind her ear.

"Take a breath, Alice. We're just getting started." Patricia patted the flustered woman's arm and then turned to face the rest of the coven. "Our most pressing matter at the moment is to establish a comprehensive training schedule for Stevie and Charlie."

Stevie rubbed her neck. "Do you really think that Charlie is ready for this?"

"Absolutely! The more he knows, the less likely he is to make a mistake. The same applies to you, my dear." She winked. "We haven't even had a chance to go over the four elements of natural magic. We'll make that a priority."

"Oh, it's been such a long time since I've had a young witch to teach." Alice clasped her hands under her chin like a young girl admiring a puppy. "This is going to be fun."

Patricia leaned forward and held Stevie's gaze. "Now, some of us have specialized gifts in addition to our general magic abilities. Deborah uses her knitting for spell work. Randy has a talent for healing as well as dream visions. Dylan can read minds, and Ruth can communicate with animals. Alice is especially skilled with plants and herbs. Much of her magic is practiced in her kitchen and her garden."

"You might say that I'm an 'old school' witch." Alice giggled.

Ruth shifted in her seat. "I'll teach you how to talk to my pit bulls when I get back to town. You'd be surprised by how much they have to say when they're not busy sniffing each other's butts."

"Thanks, Ruth. That will be very helpful." Patricia nodded and then turned back to Stevie. "It'll be good for you to learn about all of these different types of magic so you can understand the mechanics better. You might even find that you prefer one particular method over another."

A soft snore interrupted the conversation. Stevie glanced in Randy's direction to find him already napping.

Patricia coughed. "Ruth, could you wake Randy up for us?"

"Wake up, Randy!" Ruth smacked his arm.

Randy's eyes popped open, and he straightened with a start. "I'm awake!"

"I was hoping for something a little more subtle." Patricia gestured toward Randy. "But thank you."

Ruth crossed her arms. "If you want subtle, you're going to have to be more specific."

As the meeting continued, Stevie scheduled training sessions for herself and Charlie with all of the other witches. As excited as she was to learn more about the practice, she was still nervous about exposing Charlie to so much magic at his young age. He was already so powerful though. Maybe it would be a good thing to teach him how to channel all of that energy.

Patricia reminded the group of their responsibilities during the upcoming holiday season. The Historic Society had a bake sale to prepare for, as well as other charitable programs to organize. "We'll focus more on those events at our next meeting." She rose from her chair to indicate that the meeting had concluded. "Thank you all for coming today."

As the coven members stood and prepared to leave, Stevie leaned in close to Lexi. "I noticed that I wasn't scheduled to train with you at all."

Lexi grinned. "Come to think of it, Patricia has never sent anyone to me for training. I guess she doesn't consider seduction to be a specialized gift."

Alice walked up behind Lexi and cleared her throat. "That reminds me, dear. I wanted to invite you to come to church with me. You too, Stevie. The guest pastor I scheduled is really great. He's a young guy with lots of enthusiasm. I've heard that his sermons are very exciting. Are you free this Sunday?"

Lexi stared wide-eyed at Alice for a long moment as she fidgeted with one of her dangling earrings. "You know, church isn't really my thing."

Stevie squirmed as Alice's gaze transferred to her. She had nothing planned for Sunday and therefore had no excuse not to accept the invitation. She hooked her arm around Lexi's. "We'll be there!"

Lexi pursed her lips and glared.

Alice smiled. "Wonderful! You might just find that you like going to church, Lexi. Maybe you'll meet a nice young man."

"What on earth would I do with a nice man?" Lexi laughed.

Chapter seven

Stevie

Later that afternoon, Stevie arrived at Charlie's school to pick him up. As she walked through the deserted hallway, she heard the chatter of students within their classrooms. Soon, the bell would ring and the empty corridor would fill with a flood of children all rushing toward the legion of yellow school buses in the parking lot. She remembered the end-of-day excitement she'd always had as a student in this same school so many years ago. Did Charlie experience the same anticipation?

Charlie. She cringed as her thoughts drifted to his reaction to seeing her cry the night before. It had been nothing short of gut-wrenching to witness him experience a meltdown after going so long without one. She'd always attributed his progress to the dietary changes and nutritional supplements she had implemented. Now, she wondered if she'd been mistaken. What if he wasn't really improving? What if she was just getting better at preventing his exposure to triggers? She sighed.

She reached his kindergarten classroom and stood just outside the open door for a moment. Unnoticed by the students and his teacher, she scanned the room in search of her son. By default, her gaze drifted to the solitary child in the room. But it wasn't Charlie who sat unaccompanied at one of the low tables, scribbling with a crayon.

She spotted him in the far corner of the large classroom, playing alongside a little girl in pigtails. The girl smiled and placed four colorful building blocks in a row on the floor. Red, green, blue, and yellow. She pushed the box of blocks toward Charlie. He studied the contents for a moment and then began to add to the row of blocks that the girl had placed between them. He duplicated the pattern she'd created—red, green, blue, and yellow.

Stevie's heart leapt to her throat as she watched him slide the box back to the little girl. He wasn't just playing in the vicinity of another child; he was playing *with* another child.

His teacher, Maura, noticed Stevie and walked to the doorway to greet her. "He had a great day today."

Her shoulders relaxed, releasing the tension she held every time the teacher approached her with a report. Maura was a witch herself, and the mother of a child with autism, so Stevie knew she understood her concerns in a way no one else could. A "great day" not only meant that there'd been no meltdowns but also that her little witch child hadn't turned anyone into a frog.

"Thanks." Stevie beamed.

"There's a note in his take home folder. We seem to be in the midst of an early flu outbreak. We've been told that the virus has mutated, and the vaccine is completely ineffective in preventing the strain that's going around this year. There were four children absent today, and I had to send another one home early because he started running a fever." Maura cocked her head in Charlie's direction. "Keep a close eye on him, and please don't bring him to school if he has any symptoms, especially a fever."

"Of course."

chapter eight

Patricia

Patricia woke up coughing on Tuesday morning. Fighting a bone-shaking chill, she shivered and pulled the covers up to her chin. Her entire body ached. She couldn't remember ever being so sick.

Jim sat by her side. "Pat, I'm really worried. You coughed all night long, and now you're burning up with fever. We need to get you to a doctor."

She groaned. "I think this is the flu. There's nothing a doctor can do to help me."

Except for Randy, but he's out of town.

"What can I do to help? Can I make you some soup? I think we've got a can of chicken noodle in the pantry." He tucked the blanket tighter around her body.

Patricia coughed and forced a weak smile. Jim had never had to take care of her before, and he was well out of his element. "That's sweet, but I have no appetite at all."

Jim reached across her and lifted the pillow from his side of their bed. "Here, let's put this under you. Maybe it will help."

Patricia raised her head, wincing from the body aches that came with even the slightest movement. "Thank you." She sniffed. "Now, you have to leave. I don't want you to catch this."

He shook his head. "There's no way I'm leaving you here all alone."

Patricia met his gaze. "You're still recovering from that heart attack. It would be dangerous for you to catch the flu now. You can't stay here. Alice will help me." Sometimes she wished he were a member of the coven. Then he'd *have* to do as she commanded.

Jim sighed. "I'll call her. But if she can't come over, I'm staying."

Patricia gave a slight nod. She knew Alice would come to her rescue, armed with herbal remedies and maybe enough magic to lessen the misery of the virus.

She waited, shivering in bed, while Jim called Alice. Her teeth chattered from the unbearable cold that ripped through her body. Of all the times for Randy to take a vacation. She pursed her lips and considered calling him back.

No, that would be selfish. This is just the flu. It's no big deal.

Jim returned, carrying an extra blanket. He placed it on top of her and tucked the sides in close around her body. "Alice said she'd get here as soon as she could. She said something about needing a little time to gather supplies, so I'll just wait here with you until she comes."

"No. Go out on the boat with Sam, okay? I'll be fine." She wanted to him to go as far away from her germs as possible. "I'm so tired I'll probably just sleep anyway."

Jim's gray brows knitted together. "Okay. But for the record, I'm leaving under duress." He patted the mound of blankets that covered her. "You call me if you need anything, right?"

"Go, honey." Congestion rattled in her chest. "I'll be fine."

Soon after Jim left, Patricia pulled the amulet up through the collar of her nightgown. She didn't uncloak it. Instead, she simply curled her fingers around the amethyst pendant, taking comfort in its presence. Another deep cough rumbled through her, and she recalled the premonition she'd experienced weeks earlier. She closed her eyes and focused her thoughts, hoping to add details to the vague sense of foreboding. But nothing came to her.

The sudden chime of the doorbell snapped her out of her thoughts. With all the strength she could muster, she pushed herself up and stood on wobbly legs beside the bed. She leaned against the wall to steady herself amid the wave of dizziness that struck and, with great effort, trudged down the hall to the front door.

Through another bout of coughing, she managed to swing the door open and found a strange man on her porch. She struggled to catch her breath as she recovered from the hacking fit.

The man's jaw dropped as he took a small step away from the doorway, increasing the distance between them. She hadn't bothered to glance in a mirror, but she could imagine just how awful she must have looked.

The man stared at her with wide eyes. "Patricia Guthrie?"

"Yes?"

"I'm Chaplain Benjamin Parris. We have a mutual acquaintance." He paused and tugged on his shirt sleeve as though uncertain what to say next. "I wondered if I might have a few minutes of your time."

Patricia succumbed to another coughing fit, this one more forceful than the last. After a series of wheezy breaths, she composed herself. "I'm sorry. I really can't talk right now. I'm very sick." She started to close the door. "Another time, perhaps?"

Alice bustled up the walkway carrying a basket full of remedies. "What are you doing out of bed?"

Patricia heaved a sigh of relief. "Oh, thank goodness."

"I'm here, dear." Alice made her way up the porch steps. Once she reached the top, she greeted the man who stood beside the door. "Hello, I'm Alice Gillikin. I don't think I've seen you around before. Are you new to the area?"

He introduced himself once again. "Just visiting. I live in New Bern."

"Well, welcome! I think you'll enjoy Beaufort. It's quite a special town." Alice's eyes twinkled.

"That's what I hear." The chaplain continued fidgeting with his cuffs. "It was nice meeting both of you." He nodded to Patricia. "I hope you feel better soon." He stepped down onto the walkway.

"Oh, wait." Alice waved at him. "My church has a prayer meeting and a fellowship supper scheduled for tomorrow night. Would you and your family care to join us?"

If Patricia hadn't felt so awful, she might have smiled as she watched Alice's interaction with him. The senior witch had never met a stranger, and she surely never missed an opportunity to invite someone new to her church.

"Yes, ma'am. I'd like that very much." He nodded. "It'll just be me though. I don't have a family."

Alice gave him directions to her church. "See you there." She glanced at Patricia, who stood swaying in the doorway. "Goodness gracious, you *are* sick. Let's get you back in the bed."

Alice set her basket down on the foyer floor and helped Patricia walk back to her bedroom. "What was that chaplain doing here?"

"I don't know. I didn't even think to ask. Probably something for the Historic Society." Patricia shook her head. "What did he say his name was again? It was familiar, but I can't quite remember…" She succumbed to another bout of barking and hacking.

"We'll figure it out after we get this flu virus under control, okay? No need to worry about him now." Alice patted Patricia's arm. "I've brought a bunch of goodies to help you feel better. It won't work as fast as Randy's healing magic, but it'll help. I'll start you off with my special hot toddy. I make it with elderberry syrup, oil of oregano, organic lemon juice, raw honey, and some very good whiskey."

Patricia cringed. "That must have quite a flavor." She coughed again.

"Oh, it's positively horrible." Alice wrinkled her nose. "But I can fix that part. It won't be so bad. I promise." She eased Patricia back into her bed.

As another violent coughing fit seized her, Patricia's eyes watered, and she gasped for air. Several long moments passed while she struggled to catch her breath.

Wide-eyed, Alice clasped her hand over her mouth.

Patricia panted, exhausted. "What is it?"

"Oh dear." Alice wrung her hands. "Did you have a spell like that while the chaplain was here?"

Patricia thought for a moment. "Yes, why?"

"The amulet. You're too weak to keep it hidden when you cough. It was clearly visible—only for a second—but I saw it clear as day." Alice sunk down on the bed beside Patricia. "Do you think the chaplain saw it?"

"Seems like he would have said something if he noticed a large amethyst appear and disappear, don't you think?" Patricia wiped the sweat from her brow. "I'm sure he didn't see it." She tucked the amulet into her nightgown, just in case it happened again.

Chapter nine

Stevie

Stevie prepared Charlie's snack while he waited at the kitchen table. Haunted by an uneasy feeling all day, she was glad to have him home with her. She selected a red apple from the fruit bowl and rinsed it.

Though she hadn't been a witch for long, she already knew not to dismiss a nagging sense of worry out of hand, no matter how random it may seem. She'd learned that lesson the night of the hurricane when Vanessa launched her final attack. The tension in her shoulders grew tighter as she placed the apple on a cutting board and sliced it.

When Alice had called to tell her about her mother's bout with the flu, Stevie figured that was the source of her unexplained anxiety. Patricia never got sick, and with Randy out of town, she didn't have the safety net of magical healing.

Stevie swiped a thin smear of almond butter across each apple slice. Knowing the "why" of her preternatural worries had done little to ease her concern. If anything, she'd only grown more anxious as the afternoon rolled on. *Stay alert. Be ready.* She shook her head. She'd been a worrywart before her powers manifested. Now, she had the added burden of sensing troubles she didn't know she had. She sighed and placed the apple slices on the table.

Instead of playing with his tablet, Charlie sat motionless in his chair. Stevie slid the plate closer to him, but he gave it only a fleeting glance and then looked away.

Stevie cocked her head. "Charlie? Are you okay?" She watched him, waiting for a response that never came. Though he was right there in front of her, he was out of her reach. Lost in a thought he couldn't share.

Something wasn't right. She pulled his tablet out of his backpack and placed it in front of him on the table. "Can you type something for me? Anything at all?"

Charlie made no attempt to accommodate her request. Instead, he stood up from the table, abandoning his uneaten snack, and shuffled down the hall. Stevie followed him to the den where he lay on his side on the couch and stared in the direction of the dark television screen.

Stevie's heart raced. This wasn't like him at all. *Maybe he's caught the flu too.* She placed her hand on his forehead. He had no fever, but she knew he wasn't well.

It was times like this that she hated autism the most. If he could just tell her what was wrong, she could help him. The anxiety that had pestered Stevie throughout the day grew even more intense as her stomach twisted in an uneasy knot.

She decided to call the pediatrician to see if she could bring Charlie in right away. Maybe he could figure out what was wrong. She ran to the kitchen to retrieve her phone, scooped it up off the counter, and rushed right back to the den to be with Charlie again.

When she returned a few seconds later, she found that Charlie had rolled onto his back. His eyes were open, but his skin had lost all of its color. She'd never seen him so pale before.

"Charlie!" She dropped to her knees beside him. "Can you hear me?"

Stevie set her phone down on the floor. "Charlie?" She cupped his face in her hands and recoiled from the intense heat of his skin. She didn't need a thermometer to tell her that he was now running a high fever, the likes of which she had never seen before.

Her hands trembled as she stripped off his shirt in a desperate attempt to help him cool down, but the intense heat radiated from his body without mercy. It had come on so fast. He'd been fine one minute, burning up with fever the next.

Stevie snatched her phone up and dialed 911. As soon as the emergency dispatcher answered, she recited her address. In between shallow, desperate breaths, she explained what was happening as quickly as she could, as if that would somehow make help arrive faster.

She pressed her phone tight against her ear. The dispatcher said something about staying on the line, but the woman's words registered as a jumbled mess in Stevie's mind. She kept her gaze locked on Charlie, who remained still as a board. His unblinking eyes stared at nothing, wide open and vacant.

"Charlie?" Stevie gripped his arm and shook him. "Charlie, please look at me!"

A blue hue formed around his lips, stark against the pallor of skin. Stevie gasped, helpless, as the discoloration stretched across his entire face.

"He's not breathing!" She shouted into the phone. "No! No!" The phone slipped from her grasp and clattered onto the wooden floorboards.

The blue color spread onto his arms and chest, darkening with each passing moment. Her baby boy was slipping away, and she couldn't stop it. Her heart thundering in her ears, she gripped his arms, fighting with all her might to keep him with her.

Hot, blue, still. Too still.

"No, sweet baby. Stay with me." Her pleas rang out in the silence. Unheard, unanswered.

Agony ripped through her soul as she wrapped her arms around her precious child.

She raised her head to the heavens and screamed.

Chapter ten

Susan

Susan retreated to the solitude of her room after a tedious group therapy session led by Doctor Max. She closed her door and rested her back against it, pleased to have time away from the wackos who populated the ward. Those whiners were exhausting. Nightfall was still hours away, but she wished it was already time for lights out.

Just as she took a seat on the edge of her narrow bed, a knock sounded at her door. She rolled her eyes. So much for peace and quiet. "Come in."

Chaplain Parris poked his head inside the room. "Do you have a few minutes to talk?"

"All I've got is time." Susan threw her hands up. "What do you want?"

Parris walked in, leaving the door propped open behind him. He approached with an undeniable spring in his step.

"You were right." His eyes gleamed.

"Oh? Did you find Patricia?" Susan arched an eyebrow and tilted her head.

The chaplain's gaze fell on an armless metal chair in the corner. He dragged it across the room and positioned it in front of Susan. "More than that." He sat down. "I *saw* the amulet you talked about."

Susan gasped. "Well, where is it?"

"It was the strangest thing." Parris shook his head. "When I went to Patricia's home, I honestly didn't expect much, but I thought I'd talk to her and get a feel for the situation."

"What about the amulet? Where is it?" Susan gestured with her hand, urging him to hurry up with the story.

"Well, she answered the door, and boy, did she look awful. She was in the middle of a terrible coughing fit when it appeared." The chaplain moved his hands in excited waves and jabs as he spoke. "It was right there around her neck…big, purple stone on a thick, gold chain."

Susan's mouth fell open. "*It appeared?*"

He hunched forward. "Here's the kicker—it completely *disappeared* when she stopped coughing. It was there one second, gone the next. Strangest thing I've ever seen!"

"She's wearing it!" Susan slapped her hand down on her knee. "Of course! Patricia must be using some sort of disguising spell to keep it hidden. You said she was coughing. If she's sick, she might not have the strength to maintain the spell."

"Disguising spell?" He narrowed his eyes. "How is it that you know so much about her magic?"

Susan cringed. She had no choice but to provide an honest answer to his question. But she didn't have to tell him *everything*. Since he didn't have access to her records, he'd have no way of knowing about the confessions she'd laid bare to Doctor Max. "I used to be a witch myself." She paused, giving the chaplain a moment to process her truth. "But I no longer have any powers. The coven took them from me."

He sunk back in his chair as his face pinched in contempt. "It never occurred to me that you might be one of…them." He met her gaze. "I thought you hated them."

"Don't get all worked up over it." Susan gave a dismissive wave of her hand. "I don't have any powers now. I hate that coven more than you can possibly imagine."

Chaplain Parris stared down at the linoleum floor and sighed. "I feel like I have to choose between the lesser of two evils."

"There is no choice to be made. Stick with me." She rested her bony hand on her chest. "I know more about those witches than you ever will. Together, we can bring down the entire coven."

He raised his head and met her gaze. "Exactly how will we do that?"

"Bring the amulet to me."

Chapter eleven

Stevie

C harlie, come back." Stevie's hoarse voice rattled in her raw throat. "I can't lose you." Her entire body quaked as she held on to his motionless, discolored body.

Tears streamed unfettered down her cheeks as she struggled to comprehend losing him. A life without Charlie was no life at all. He was her everything.

She could stop a speeding car with a thought. She could blow up a boat with a blast of her powerful energy. But there was nothing—nothing—she could do to save her son. Her magic roiled within her, useless.

There must be something...

A sudden flash of memory jolted her out of her grief-stricken stupor. She snapped her head up, glimpsing his vacant stare as she scooped him off the couch. His small body still burned with fever as she positioned him on the floor.

How long had it been since he'd taken a breath? She didn't know. Each second had passed as a hellish eternity.

She pressed on, remembering her lifeguard training. "Airway. Breathing. Circulation." She recited the order aloud to keep

71

herself focused on the task at hand and began to move through the steps she'd learned as a teenager. She lifted Charlie's chin and tilted his head back to open his airway.

Bending over him, she pinched his nostrils closed. She filled her own lungs with air and then exhaled it into her son's mouth. His chest rose and fell and then lay flat once more. She did it again. Nothing changed.

Airway. Breathing. Circulation.

Placing two trembling fingers on his carotid artery, Stevie held her own breath while she searched for his pulse. If she couldn't find it, she'd have to begin chest compressions. The muted wail of a siren rang out in the distance.

Please, Charlie. Please hang on.

She detected his pulse. It was slow and weak, but it was there. She studied his chest for any sign of movement. Nothing. He still wasn't breathing.

Drawing in another great gulp of air, she pinched his nose, closed her mouth over his, and pushed the breath from her lungs into his body. She counted off the seconds as she leaned over his face, listening and watching for any sign of breathing. One, two, three, four, five. Then she delivered yet another rescue breath.

A slight movement caught her eye, and she jerked back to get a better view of Charlie's chest. She waited, willing the movement to happen again as the shriek of the siren outside grew louder.

Charlie's eyes closed as he began to draw in his own breaths. The blue hue that covered his body receded, fading and shrinking until only the pale tone of his flesh remained.

She scooped his limp body into her arms and raced out the front door to meet the ambulance, which had just pulled up. Its siren stopped blaring, but its lights continued to flash as two emergency medical technicians jumped out. Stevie ran toward them. One held out his arms to take Charlie.

A third technician approached her. He nodded toward her open front door. "Anybody else at home?"

Unable to speak, Stevie shook her head.

"I'll take care of it." The technician continued past her.

The clarity she'd experienced while she worked to save Charlie gave way to the numbness of shock. Detached from the activity surrounding her, she moved forward on instinct, following the EMT who carried Charlie.

She watched, in a dreamlike daze, as he placed Charlie on a gurney and strapped an oxygen mask to his face. One of the technicians offered his hand to help her step into the vehicle. Without a word, she took it and climbed in.

She sat down on a bench next to Charlie. He looked so small on the gurney, so very fragile. She raised a shaking hand to her mouth, stifling a cry.

She stared at her son's face and spoke to no one in particular. "He stopped breathing. He turned blue." Tears welled in her eyes, but her voice remained calm, almost robotic. "His eyes were open, but he wasn't there. He was gone."

He was gone.

A technician pulled the ambulance doors closed. "He's running a high fever, but he's breathing fine now." He said those words as if this happened every day, as if Charlie had endured nothing more than a paper cut.

The ambulance pulled away. Stevie squeezed Charlie's hand, grateful for each breath he took in.

Fractured pictures flashed in her mind. The haunting blue hue that marched across his face. His blank stare. She clutched her stomach as a wave of nausea struck. She'd almost lost him. It was her worst fear realized, but somehow she'd broken through the terror and saved him.

I saved him.

She stroked the soft skin of Charlie's hand with her thumb and closed her eyes. He was the center of every defining point of her life. The day of his birth, when she became a mother. The day he received his autism diagnosis, when she became determined. And now this, the day he stopped breathing…when she became fierce.

Chapter twelve

Alice

A lice walked across the parking lot to her church on Wednesday evening. A fast moving cold front was zipping through, turning summer into fall with each new gust of wind. She shivered and pulled her sweater closed.

She climbed onto the front step of the two-hundred-year-old building and stood just to the right of its massive wooden doors. Since it was still a bit early, she decided to wait for Chaplain Parris outside.

Alice loved her small church. She'd witnessed countless weddings, funerals, and baptisms within its walls over the decades. She'd heard prayers offered up and watched sins be forgiven. Knowing this church would continue on long after she was gone buoyed her heart.

A gust of wind rattled the thick, waxy leaves of the magnolia trees, which stood in an elegant line along the walkway. Though they were an impressive sight in their unadorned state, Alice looked forward to the grand white blooms that would blossom in the spring.

A white-haired couple made their way toward the church entrance.

The woman greeted Alice with a cheerful nod. "Good evening."

"Hello, Francine." Alice glanced at the woman's husband. "Paul, it's wonderful to see you here tonight. It's been quite a while since we've had the pleasure of your company."

Paul grimaced. "Francine told me she wasn't going to cook for me tonight. She said if I wanted to eat, I'd have to come here for the spaghetti supper after the prayer meeting."

"Is that so?" Alice raised an eyebrow. "Well, we're happy to have you with us, whatever the reason." She offered a conspiratorial wink and a grin to Francine. Some folks just needed a little extra nudge to come to church.

Francine tugged on Paul's arm. "Come on. Let's go inside. It's getting cold out here."

As the elderly couple shuffled into the church, Alice spotted Chaplain Parris heading her way. She waved and waited for him to join her on the front steps.

"I'm so glad you could make it." She patted his arm. "Let's go on in and find a seat."

He followed Alice into the modest sanctuary. The pews, original to the structure, were almost black from years of wear and refinishing. Narrow, stained glass windows lined the sides of the room, and a large cross hung high on the wall behind the altar. Hymnals and bibles were scattered among the pews for parishioners to use.

Echoes of coughs, whispers, and polite greetings drifted around the sparsely filled sanctuary as Alice and her guest proceeded down the aisle. She found her usual spot, the third pew on the right, and gestured for the chaplain to have a seat. With a quick look around, she smiled and waved at the familiar faces awaiting the start of the service, and then sat down next to him.

He cleared his throat. "How's Patricia doing? Feeling better, I hope."

"She's improved some. But this year's flu not only showed up early in the season, it's particularly severe. Patricia won't even let her husband stay in the house with her because she's afraid that he'll catch it too."

His eyebrows rose, creasing his forehead. "She's all alone?"

Alice nodded. "I'll check in on her until she's well again. She slept most of the day today. There really isn't much that anyone can do for her right now." Alice neglected to mention that she'd added valerian root to Patricia's hot toddies to help her sleep through the worst of the illness. "It's sweet of you to ask about her."

More churchgoers entered the sanctuary and found their places in the pews. Among them was a stocky, middle-aged woman who took a seat behind Alice.

The woman leaned forward and tapped Alice's shoulder. "Who's your friend?" She tilted her chin toward the chaplain, showing all of her teeth in a broad, shudder-inducing smile.

With reluctance, Alice introduced Parris to Lynne. The woman was a chronic busybody, so Alice tried to avoid her whenever possible. By bringing an unknown guest to church with her, she'd poured chum in the water, and Lynne had already begun to circle.

"So, do you live here in Beaufort?" Lynne's bangles clanked together as she gestured to him. "I don't believe I've seen you before."

"I'm from New Bern." Chaplain Parris shook his head. "I'm just visiting the area."

"That doesn't sound like a New Bern accent to me." Lynne wagged her finger, playful but insistent. "In fact, I don't think you're from North Carolina at all." She placed one hand on her hip and tilted her head as she awaited his reply.

"I'm sorry. I guess I should have been more specific. I'm *originally* from Massachusetts."

Alice admired the ease with which he handled Lynne's grilling. Surely, this wasn't the first time he'd encountered someone like her.

Satisfied with his response, Lynne launched a new line of questions. "And where is your family?" She glanced around the sanctuary as if a wife and children should accompany every adult male.

He shifted in the pew. "I'm not married."

"I see." Unbidden sympathy dripped from her words. "Where do you work? Are you with the military?"

"No. I work at a hospital."

Alice wondered what Lynne's next question would be. Perhaps she'd want to know where he went to school or why he was in town. Maybe she would ask why he was still single. She wouldn't be surprised if Lynne asked the poor man for his social security number and blood type. Just as the nosy parishioner opened her mouth to continue her interrogation, a deacon stepped up to the altar to begin the service. Alice and the chaplain turned to face the front of the church, leaving Lynne to stew in her own curiosity.

After the deacon opened the service with a prayer, the congregation stood and sang a familiar hymn of praise. When everyone settled back into their pews, he opened the floor and asked if there were any prayer requests. Several hands shot up right away, and the deacon called on each person one by one.

Time and again, prayers were asked for family members and neighbors who had come down with the flu. Many among the very old and the very young had already been hospitalized due to complications.

My goodness. It's spreading fast. As Alice looked around the sanctuary, she caught a glimpse of movement behind her. From the corner of her eye, she saw Lynne wave her hand with a particular sense of urgency.

Oh dear. Alice cringed. Lynne used prayer requests to humblebrag, spread rumors, and create drama like it was an art form.

Lynne rose from the pew and smoothed her skirt. "Thank you, Deacon." She beamed as if she were receiving an award.

Alice felt Lynne's gaze fall upon her, and she knew the woman wouldn't be satisfied with a sideways glance. Taking the less-than-subtle hint, Alice twisted around in her seat to face the busybody.

"I have a prayer request of a different nature, Deacon. Now, I do not intend to take away from the terrible suffering of those who have the flu. I assure you, I am not without sympathy." Lynne's smile faltered, and she held her hand over her heart. "But today, I would like to ask for your prayers for my friend who is struggling with her husband's many, many infidelities. It's just *awful.*" She paused, taking a moment to scan the expressions on the attendees' faces. "I mean, there were a *whole lot* of indiscretions on his part, and she just found out about all of them. Well, at least she *thinks* she knows about all of them. But how can she ever be sure of that? Can you believe it?" She worked the room as though she expected applause at the end of her request. "She had no idea what her own husband had been up to. Bless her heart."

The deacon cleared his throat. Alice knew he was trying to move the service along, but Lynne frowned at the interruption.

"Given the, uh, delicate nature of this request, I think it's best if I don't mention her name." Lynne sat back down in a hurry.

Alice fought the urge to roll her eyes as she turned back around to face the front of the sanctuary. Prayer meetings served a great purpose in their church community. But they also provided a most efficient venue for spreading juicy news without technically committing the sin of gossip. Lynne had become a master of utilizing that particular biblical loophole. She'd be the most popular person at the fellowship supper that evening as some of the members of the congregation tried to glean the identity of the mystery woman for whom they'd been asked to pray. Alice knew Lynne would offer up whatever information she'd held back during the service so they could all lift the poor woman up by name—with as many *specific* details as possible.

Alice planned to say a special prayer for Lynne's friend. She didn't need any more information than what she already had in order to do it.

The prayer meeting continued. The deacon noted all of the announcements of births and deaths, lost jobs and found jobs, ailing family members, and upcoming surgeries. When the congregation fell silent, he led the group in a long-winded prayer. As he read the lengthy list of flu patient names, Alice thought of Patricia. She knew her queen didn't think much of prayer, but she offered up a silent invocation anyway.

Having handled the primary business of the meeting, the deacon looked to Alice. "Do you have any announcements to add before we go?"

"Yes, Deacon." Alice stood and addressed the congregation. "As you all know, our pastor is suffering with the flu. I had arranged for another pastor to fill in for him this week, but, unfortunately, he has also just fallen ill. So, at this point, we don't have anyone to deliver the sermon this Sunday morning. If someone doesn't volunteer to do it, then I'll have to do it. And, I don't think anyone wants to see that happen." She chuckled, and the congregation laughed along with her. "I'll be at the fellowship supper tonight. If you can help, please let me know." She returned to her seat.

The deacon nodded, acknowledging Alice's announcement. "I'm sorry to say that I'll be out of town this weekend. Otherwise, I'd be glad to step up." He scanned the congregation. "Surely someone will feel led to fill in for our pastor under these unusual circumstances."

Nearly an hour after it started, the prayer service ended. Alice and Chaplain Parris rose from their pew.

"Alice, I'm sorry to hear about all of the illness that has plagued your church family." He smoothed his tie. "I would be happy to help by delivering the sermon on Sunday."

"Oh, that would be wonderful. Thank you so much!" Alice smiled, relieved. "I assumed you most likely had responsibilities of your own on Sunday morning, so I didn't ask. Are you sure you don't mind?"

"It's no trouble at all." Chaplain Parris waved away her concern. "In fact, it will be my pleasure to speak to your congregation."

Chapter Thirteen

Stevie

Stevie followed the medical technicians as they wheeled Charlie into a room in the bustling emergency department. As soon as they positioned his gurney on the back wall, she rushed to his side and squeezed his limp hand. His skin still burned hot with fever.

One of the EMTs stepped into the doorway and spoke to someone whose face Stevie could not see. She heard him relay the information she'd given him about Charlie, but then he began to talk in a series of abbreviations and numbers. Medical lingo. She didn't know what any of it meant.

A red-haired nurse hurried into the room and whipped the stethoscope from around her neck. Without a word, she began to check Charlie's vital signs. Stevie watched her work. She had a million questions, each one swirling in her mind like acrylic paint in water, but none of them made it to her lips. She gazed down at her son. His eyes remained closed, and the fringe of his long, blond lashes rested against his chubby cheeks. He looked just like he was sleeping.

The medical technicians began to file out of the room. Stevie wanted to thank them for their help, but she could only manage a soft whisper.

The last one heard her and faced her with a kind grin. "Try not to worry. They'll take good care of him here." He patted the foot of the gurney and left.

Stevie's gaze drifted around the small room while the nurse continued her assessment. It was identical to the one her father had been in after he suffered his heart attack just a few weeks earlier. Visiting her father in the emergency department had been gut-wrenching enough. It was a thousand times more difficult to be there with Charlie.

Her senses, heightened by the onset of her magical abilities, protested against the onslaught of sights, sounds, and smells of the emergency area. It was too bright, too busy, and the smell of antiseptic was too strong. She heard random coughs and loud cries coming from multiple locations within the department. She closed her eyes for a long moment. *Charlie would hate this.* She gazed at his face once again and tried to block out the misery that surrounded them.

"His temperature is a little over one-oh-four. Everything else is normal." The nurse tapped a button on the monitor. "The doctor will be in shortly." She left the room.

Stevie pulled a chair next to the gurney and sat down. He'd never run a fever this high before, and she had no idea what it meant. Her vision blurred as a fresh batch of tears rolled down her cheeks.

"Mrs. Lewis?" A tall woman in a white lab coat entered the room. "I'm Doctor Bennet. Can you tell me what happened with your son?" She passed a small box of thin, stiff tissues to Stevie.

"Thank you." Stevie dried her tears and relayed the story to the doctor. Though she didn't speak of the agony she'd endured at the sight of her lifeless child, she was unable to rein in the tremble in her voice as the memory flashed in her mind. "I gave him four rescue breaths. He started breathing on his own after that."

"Good job." The doctor's eyebrows rose. "How did you know to do that?"

"I used to be lifeguard. It was part of the training." Stevie glanced back at Charlie. "I didn't think to do it right away though. I panicked." A fresh lump formed in her throat. "I don't know how much time I wasted before I remembered what to do."

"Probably not as long as you think. Time moves differently in situations like this. A minute can seem like an hour." Doctor Bennet clapped a hand on Stevie's shoulder. "Don't be so hard on yourself. I'd say panic is normal under these circumstances. The important thing is that you were able to get past it." She met Stevie's gaze with a smile, and then she walked around to the other side of the gurney. "Sounds like he had a seizure." She pressed her stethoscope to his chest and listened for a moment. "Has he ever had one before?"

"No." Stevie shook her head. "Are you sure? He was completely still. He wasn't convulsing at all."

"Some seizures are like that. I suspect this one was caused by his fever." Doctor Bennet draped her stethoscope around her neck. "It could very well be an isolated incident. Febrile seizures are common in young children, and they're usually harmless. We'll do a head CT just to be thorough. But first, we're going to try to bring his fever down. Poor kid probably has the flu."

Stevie exhaled the breath she didn't realize she'd been holding and relaxed her shoulders. Throughout the entire ordeal with Charlie that afternoon, she'd never guessed that he had been having a seizure. Between his still body, blue skin, and that horrible empty stare, she'd assumed the worst. It was a small comfort to know the truth of what had happened. Still, she wasn't sure the torment of seeing her son like that could ever be undone.

She stared at Charlie's face. More than anything, she wanted to see his bright blue eyes full of life once again. "How long do you think he'll be unconscious?"

"Oh, he's just sleeping. Seizures are exhausting." Doctor Bennet gave a nonchalant wave. "I wouldn't be surprised if he slept until morning." She finished examining Charlie and left.

Stevie leaned over her son and planted a kiss on his forehead. "I love you."

Realizing she still needed to call Sam, Stevie reached into her pocket for her cell phone. It wasn't there. In the chaos, she'd forgotten to bring it with her. She spotted a telephone mounted on the wall and picked up the receiver.

Finger poised over the keypad, she hesitated. They hadn't spoken since she broke the news to him that she was seeing Dylan. She dialed the number and listened as the call went to his voicemail. After the beep, she explained what had happened with Charlie, struggling all the way through to keep the torrent of emotion from revealing itself in her voice.

Chapter fourteen

Susan

As Susan prepared for bed, her heart still raced with excitement over the chaplain's revelation about the amulet. Between that and the new alertness that came from not taking her daily medications, she knew sleep wouldn't come easy for her. She glanced at her trash bin, where she'd hidden the last dose of pills she'd feigned swallowing.

Maybe I could take one—just to take the edge off. She shook away the idea almost as soon as it entered her mind. All that mattered now was keeping a clear head. She had to take great care with the chaplain, and she had to keep her edge. Navigating the muddy waters of her truth-telling curse, along with his witch obsession, had proven more challenging than she'd anticipated. One misstep and the entire plan could fall out of her favor. She had to stay in control of herself so she could control him. She'd sleep when she got out of the hospital.

Susan selected a clean set of pajamas from her bureau. Though there wasn't much difference between the loungewear she donned during the day and the pajamas she wore at night, she held to the ritual of changing her clothes before bed. Most of the patients in the ward never bothered to change their attire for sleeping. In fact, some of them often went several days without changing their clothes at all. But *those* people belonged in this hospital. Susan did not. She twisted the cotton fabric in her hands until her knuckles turned white. She was only in this awful place because of the coven.

Taking a deep breath, she released her grip on the fabric. *It won't be long now. They will pay for this.*

She dressed and slipped on a terry bathrobe over her pajamas. It, like everything else in Susan's current wardrobe, was a second hand item donated to the hospital by a local charity. The aqua robe was in good condition and showed minimal signs of wear. Its only flaw was the embroidered picture on the hemline—a brown puppy with floppy ears.

Ridiculous.

Susan recalled Vanessa's pitiful pleas as a young girl, her constant begging for a puppy of her own. She'd always rejected the incessant requests. The last thing she had wanted was for her daughter to become soft and weak while cuddling some silly little animal.

Someone knocked on her door.

"Come in."

The door creaked open, and Chaplain Parris stepped in to her room. "Good evening, Susan."

"It's late. What are you doing here?" She placed her hands on her hips and tilted her head. "Do you have the amulet?"

"No." He shook his head. "Not yet." He smiled in spite of his failure.

Susan sighed and took a seat on the edge of her bed. "Then what do you want?"

"I just left a church service that I attended with Alice Gillikin. Do you know her? She's a friend of Patricia's."

Susan laughed. "Congratulations, Chaplain. You just went to church with a witch."

The chaplain's eyes bulged and his jaw dropped. "Alice is a witch too? Are you sure?"

"She's not just any witch. She's a member of the coven." Susan smirked. "I told you that there are literally hundreds of witches in Beaufort. They're everywhere. You have no idea how pervasive they are."

"But she's a leader in her church, for goodness' sake." Chaplain Parris shook his head. "These witches defy everything we've learned about their kind throughout history. They should live on the fringes of society, hiding their shameful ways. But no, they live freely among the innocent people of the town." He scowled and began to pace.

Susan stifled a grin as she watched his reaction. The angrier he got, the better. "And you never would have known about them if it weren't for me."

The chaplain continued to pace. His black tasseled loafers squeaked against the linoleum with each step. "With hundreds of them on the loose, they may very well have infiltrated every element of that small town. Teachers, doctors, shopkeepers— anyone could be guilty." He ran a hand through his thinning hair. "What's even more disturbing is the thought that they may have taken posts within the local government. If any of the judges and politicians are tainted, it will be more difficult to legalize the elimination of witches."

"*Elimination*? Is that meant to be a polite way of saying public hangings or burning witches at the stake?" Susan let out a low whistle. "Have you told anyone other than me about your desire to bring back the executions?"

"Of course not." The chaplain threw his head back and stared at the ceiling for a long moment. "It's not the sort of thing I should talk openly about. Not yet, anyway. First, I have to light the fires of fear within the community, just like my ancestors did. I must explain to the masses why they should be afraid. The idea won't seem so crazy once there's growing support for it. And with the flu outbreak in full-swing, they're already scared and worried—making this a prime time to tell them about the witches in their midst."

Not crazy at all. Susan bit her lip, struggling to hold back a laugh. She wanted to keep the chaplain angry, just not at her.

He met Susan's gaze. "I can share all of this with you because no one would believe you if you repeated it. A mental health patient is not exactly a trusted source of information."

Susan's amusement vanished, and she hung her head. *No one would believe you.* She'd heard that before. The coven had counted on that very fact when they locked her away in the psychiatric hospital. No one had believed her claims of the truth-telling spell. And her ravings that the honorable members of the Beaufort Historic Society had been behind her imprisonment had only earned her a sedative shot. She rubbed her hip, remembering the sting of the thick needle.

She took a deep breath. Knowing she had to keep her anger in check if she was going to make this alliance work, she held her head upright once again.

"Look, I didn't say that to hurt your feelings." Chaplain Parris raised his hands as if to calm a crowd. "My own father spent some time in a mental health facility. He's the one who taught me to be careful who I shared this…interest with."

The chaplain's acknowledgement of his family history confirmed Susan's suspicions. He was indeed worthy of joining the ranks of patients in this hospital. She closed her eyes for a moment, reminding herself to proceed with care. His instability might just be her greatest asset.

She tilted her head in posed nonchalance. "What happens next?"

"I have volunteered to be a guest speaker at Alice's church on Sunday. I'll use that time to begin laying the groundwork for a revolt against the witches in town. Subtlety will be key, of course." He grinned.

"I'm not really a fan of subtlety myself. If you want to start a witch hunt, why not put it all out there?"

The chaplain paced the length of the room again. "If I go in there ranting about witches, the moderate parishioners are likely to tune out. I might even find myself an unwilling guest in this facility if one of them decides to call the authorities. I'll start with simply planting the seeds of fear and doubt. I can do that without even mentioning the witches." He stopped and faced Susan. "It takes time to turn a community around. This is only the beginning."

"What about the amulet?"

"I'll take care of that too." He gave a sharp nod. "I plan to get it tomorrow. Are you sure that thing will give us the upper hand against the coven?"

"Absolutely."

Chapter Fifteen

Stevie

Stevie held Charlie's hand as he lay sleeping in the emergency department. She studied the soft features of his face. His fever had come down, and his color had almost returned to normal. He was still a little pale, but no trace of the haunting blue hue lingered around his mouth or his fingertips. She stroked his cheek, knowing she should be more relieved than she was. But she longed to see life in his bright eyes again. Nothing would convince her that he was truly okay until he woke up and she could see it for herself. She brushed a wayward blond curl from his forehead.

A petite technician entered the room. "Mrs. Lewis, it's time for Charlie's CT scan."

"Oh, okay." Stevie rose from her seat by Charlie's bedside. She rubbed the knot in her neck and stretched. A couple of hours of sitting had left her body stiff, so she was glad to have the opportunity to move around a bit. She stepped toward the doorway.

"You'll have to wait in here." The technician raised her hand to stop her. "This won't take long." She unlocked the wheels on the gurney and rolled Charlie out of the room.

In the solitude, Stevie realized how exhausted she was. She'd worked so hard to be strong in the face of her worst fear, she hadn't realized how hard it had been on her—until now. She took in a deep breath and let it out with a slow exhale. She tried, without success, to shake the tension out of her shoulders.

She wished there was some way she could get in touch with Dylan. He had a gift for easing her worries, and she needed that now more than ever.

The technician returned with Charlie, who was still asleep in spite of his trip through the busy emergency department. She pushed his gurney back into place, locked its wheels, and left the room with nothing more than a nod in Stevie's direction.

Stevie settled back into the uncomfortable chair at Charlie's bedside and wrapped her hand around his once more. She glanced at the wall-mounted phone. Sam hadn't called back yet. She knew he wouldn't let his anger get in the way of being with Charlie now, so he must be too busy to check his voicemail. If he didn't call soon, she'd have to try again.

Doctor Bennet came back, carrying a file. "Charlie's CT scan looks normal, but he has tested positive for the flu. It's probably safe for him to go home, but I'd like to admit him for an overnight stay given the severity of his seizure."

Stevie nodded. As much as she wanted to bring Charlie home and get back to their version of normal, she was terrified that he might have another seizure. "Thank you, Doctor Bennet."

The doctor left the room, and soon, an orderly came in to take Charlie up to the pediatric floor. Without a word, Stevie followed them to the elevator.

The pediatric floor provided a stark contrast to the bustling emergency department. Given the late hour, Stevie suspected that most of the young patients in the unit were already sleeping. Except for the occasional cough or stray beeps of medical equipment, the corridor remained quiet. The orderly pushed Charlie's gurney down the cheerfully decorated hallway and into a private room.

Stevie stopped at the sink across from Charlie's bed and took a moment to splash some cold water on her face. It did little to help perk her up, but it was better than nothing. The sound of heavy footsteps came rushing down the hallway. She had no need to look outside of the room; she knew who was heading her way.

Chapter sixteen

Stevie

Sam rushed into the hospital room. Wide-eyed and flushed, he glanced from Stevie to Charlie and back to Stevie again. "Is he okay?"

She froze in place, torn between the desire to hug him and the urge to yell at him for taking so long to get there. She shook off those thoughts. He was here now, and that was all that mattered. "He's been asleep since the seizure, but the doctor said that's to be expected. He does have the flu though. So, he's at risk of having another if the medicine they gave him doesn't control his fever."

Sam nodded, stepped to Charlie's bedside, and took their son's hand in his. "I came as soon as I got your message." He glanced up at her. "I was on the boat."

"That's what I figured." Stevie looked away from him and focused her attention on Charlie.

"You said that he stopped breathing." Sam spoke slowly as if he were still trying to process all that she'd said in her voicemail. "He could have—." He stopped and swallowed hard. "You saved him, Stevie. You saved our son."

Stevie squeezed her eyes closed as the all-too-vivid memory of Charlie's discolored and still body came to the forefront of her mind. A lump grew in her throat. She opened her mouth to speak, only to close it again. If she tried to talk about it, she knew she would fall apart.

"Oh, Stevie. Are you okay? I didn't think about what this must have been like for you."

Stevie opened her eyes but kept her head down, avoiding Sam's gaze. She nodded and waved her hand in an attempt to assure him that she was all right.

"Hey, I'm here. For both of you." Sam let go of Charlie's hand and walked around the bed. "Do you want to talk about it?"

Stevie sighed. That was a monumental offer coming from Sam. He didn't like to talk about much of anything, unless it involved fishing or surfing. She wanted to tell him everything she'd witnessed, as if it would somehow lessen the torture of her recurring memories. But she wouldn't do it, she couldn't bring herself to share those images with him. The last thing she wanted was to inflict this pain on Sam.

Hot tears welled in her eyes as the image of Charlie's seizure flashed in her mind again. Blue skin. Rigid body. That vacant stare.

Sam wrapped his strong arms around her, and she rested her head on his shoulder. It was a comfortable feeling, familiar and safe. In an instant, her guard fell, and she began to sob. "It was just horrible, Sam."

He stroked her hair. "I'm so sorry."

After several moments, she lifted her head from his shoulder and wiped the salty stream of tears from her face. "I'm okay. Really."

Sam let her go, but he remained by her side. If he was still angry with her, he showed no sign of it. If anything, he was just as much the loving partner he'd been during the early days of their marriage.

"Do you want to take a break? Maybe go get some coffee or something?" Sam rubbed her arm "I can stay with him."

"No, I really can't leave him." Stevie shook her head. "But there's no need for both of us to stay here." She glanced around the small room, spotted a vinyl recliner, and nodded in its direction. "I think that'll be my bed tonight."

"Are you hungry? I can bring you something to eat." Sam raised his eyebrows. "I saw a vending machine downstairs with some really sketchy looking sandwiches. They might be almost edible." He flashed his crooked grin.

"I couldn't eat anything right now. Thanks anyway."

"No problem. Is there anything I can do?"

"The doctor said it'll just be an overnight stay. Would you mind coming back to pick us up in the morning?"

"Of course."

An awkward silence fell between them. Stevie flicked her gaze around the room. She looked at Charlie, the floor, the monitor...everywhere but Sam's eyes.

He clapped his hands together. "Well, I guess I'll get going then." He didn't move from his spot beside the bed.

She forced herself to meet his gaze. "Thanks for coming."

He swept his shaggy hair out of his eyes. "Look, I know this is weird." He glanced down at Charlie. "But we can handle this. We can still be good parents even if we aren't together anymore."

Stevie stood still, letting Sam's words wash over her. The tightness in her shoulders let go, and she smiled. "Yes. We sure can."

Sam planted a kiss on Charlie's forehead before starting toward the door.

Stevie watched his broad shoulders as he walked away, but she caught a movement out of the corner of her eye. She glanced back down at Charlie and saw his head move, lolling toward her. "Sam, wait! He just moved; maybe he's waking up."

Sam hurried back to his side of the hospital bed, and they both watched as Charlie woke up. Stevie held her breath. She couldn't wait to see life in her son's eyes once again.

She pressed her hand against her racing heart as she caught a glimpse of his pale blue irises before he began to squint and blink. She knew right away that the overhead fluorescent lights were bothering him, so she rushed to the switch beside the door. But before she reached it, all of the lights in the room went out on their own.

Stevie gasped. Charlie hadn't realized that Sam was in the room, or if he did, he was too confused at the moment to remember not to use magic in front of his dad.

"Magic." Charlie croaked out the word in a hoarse whisper.

"Stevie! Did you hear that? He spoke!" Sam grabbed her and squeezed her in a fierce hug. "Can you believe it?"

"No, I...I really can't." Stevie kept her face buried in Sam's chest, hiding the blush that burned on her cheeks. As much as she wanted to share his excitement, this was not how she'd hoped he would hear Charlie's first word. She pulled away and returned to the bedside, prepared to prevent any further magical slip ups.

"What an interesting first word." Sam tilted his head. "I wonder where that came from."

Stevie wrung her hands, seeking a plausible explanation while wishing she could just tell Sam the truth. She glanced toward the door and noticed the lights were still on in the hall-way. At least Charlie didn't knock out the electricity for the whole hospital.

She shrugged. "Maybe he thought the power outage was magical."

"Yeah, that makes sense." Sam nodded. "Charlie, that's not magic. It looks like the power is only out in this room. So it's probably just a tripped breaker or a blown fuse. Can you say *fuse*?"

Charlie did not respond. Instead, he coughed and let his con-fused gaze drift around the room.

"You're in the hospital." Stevie smoothed his hair with a lov-ing stroke of her hand. "You got very sick today, so we came here to help you get better."

Charlie yawned and closed his eyes, drifting off to sleep again.

Sam beamed at Stevie. "What do you think he'll say next?"

Stevie pressed her lips together. *Coven? Witchcraft? My grandma is the queen?* At this point, it could be anything. She shook off the thought and shrugged. "Your guess is as good as mine."

When Sam left for the night, Stevie settled into the vinyl re-cliner to rest her eyes for a bit. She heard Charlie cough a cou-ple more times before exhaustion overcame her and pulled her into a deep sleep.

Chapter seventeen

Vanessa

Vanessa lay in the dim light of the hospital room. Sunrise was still a few hours away, but she couldn't sleep.

Her mind raced with worry about where she would go next. The doctor had been in to see her on Wednesday and said he was pleased with her progress. He'd mentioned that the hospital was filling up with flu patients, and at this point, he considered her well enough to go home. But home was a cross country flight away, and she couldn't imagine making that journey in her condition. Even her bottomless bank account couldn't secure her a space in the facility when there were others who needed the room more than she did.

After her conversation with the doctor, a nurse had come to remove her morphine pump, limiting her pain relief to doses of narcotics at regular intervals. The pills dulled some of the aches, but the absence of the morphine left her more alert and more aware of her circumstances. She cast a wistful glance to the spot where the medication pump once stood. She missed it already.

The nurse had removed most of her bandages as well. Her gruesome scars did not require the same level of protection as raw, burned flesh.

Without the burden of the IV and bandages, she was somewhat confident that she could manage her own care once she left the hospital. She supposed that was a good thing because she had no one to call on for help if she needed it.

Vanessa had lived a solitary life since high school. There'd been no friendships or even a single meaningful romantic relationship. She'd stayed alone, honing her craft for the day when she could vindicate her mother. The mother who wanted nothing to do with her now.

She hadn't realized just how alone she really was until she'd endured her mother's wrath over her failure to retrieve the amulet. Closing her eyes, she replayed the conversation in her mind. Susan had shown no concern for her injuries, nor had she offered any wishes for a speedy recovery. Her own mother had not uttered a single encouraging word to help her through all that she'd suffered.

Why had she tried so hard to earn Susan's love? She'd done terrible things on her mother's behalf. For what? She'd gained nothing and lost everything—and she'd have to live with the consequences for the rest of her life. Her solitary, miserable life.

When Vanessa sensed movement in the room, she opened her eyes, expecting to see a nurse. Instead, she spotted a familiar little boy wearing a hospital gown. She gasped.

Stevie's son stood in the middle of her room.

"What are you doing here?" Recalling the boy's shocking power, her mouth went dry, and she pushed herself up against her pillow. Her eyes darted from him to the open door. She wasn't strong enough to run from him. And, without her magic, she couldn't defend herself if he decided to attack.

I'm trapped.

Charlie said nothing as he stepped closer to her bedside. His eyes flicked up to meet her gaze, but then he looked away.

Vanessa held her breath. He could end her life in an instant if he wanted to. Her heart raced in the hollowness of her chest; its thunderous echo resounded in her ears.

His mother had to be somewhere close by. She glanced at the open door again. The hallway was empty, but she knew it wouldn't stay that way for long.

"Your mom wouldn't want you in here with me." Vanessa forced her voice to stay steady. "You should go now."

Charlie remained beside her bed as if he hadn't heard her. With a furrowed brow, he studied the scars on her face and scalp. His frown deepened, reflecting her own emotions, as if he too endured the depth of her despair.

Vanessa waited for him to say something, anything. If he was angry, he showed no sign of it. In fact, she detected no animosity from this boy who was the child of her enemy. In spite of the terror she'd subjected him to, he exuded only compassion and curiosity.

It occurred to her that she'd never heard Charlie speak. Perhaps he was unable to. She didn't know much about children, but there was something unusual about this kid—something more than just his magical gift. There was a certain kindness, a purity of heart, which seemed to emanate from him. Drawn to his light, she found his presence soothing. Her fear subsided.

"Don't worry about me, kid. I'll be all right." Vanessa gave a slight wave of her unburned hand. "For what it's worth, I think I got exactly what I deserved."

Charlie's gaze flicked up to meet her own. Just as before, he glanced away in an instant. She couldn't blame him for that. She didn't want to look at herself either.

Charlie placed his hand on her arm, offering a simple comfort she'd never received from anyone before. An unexpected tear slid down her cheek, but she didn't bother to wipe it away.

Her skin tingled beneath his hand, subtle at first, but then it surged with the unmistakable energy of magic. The regret that had settled somewhere in the depths of her soul rushed forward as she remembered hurling the silver car toward him. "I'm sorry I scared you." More tears fell. She couldn't stop them.

A sudden burst of peace washed over her, and the guilt subsided almost as soon as she'd become aware of it. She blinked and wiped her face, grateful for the relief.

The boy continued to rest his hand on her arm. Vanessa's throat tightened as her blackest emotions roiled within her. One by one, they each rose up—rage, envy, greed, hate—only to fade in an instant. When light finally pierced the darkness, a hopeful sensation blossomed in her heart. She pressed her hand against her chest. She didn't know this feeling. *Friendship? Love?*

The image of her mother's angry sneer flashed in her mind, terrifying and familiar.

Weakness. This is weakness. Vanessa twisted in her bed, fighting the foreign sensation that grew within her. *No!* She wanted her anger back. She wanted to hold on to her hate. She was strongest in the darkness. She couldn't let Charlie pull her toward the light.

"No!" Vanessa jerked away from his grasp.

Charlie kept his head down but let go of her. "Magic."

Before Vanessa could respond, a nurse burst into the room. "There you are! Oh Charlie, you can't wander around the hospital by yourself." She took his hand. "Come on, let's get you back in bed before your mother wakes up."

Charlie followed the woman out the door, but he glanced back at Vanessa once more before leaving the room.

Chapter eighteen

Patricia

Patricia lay alone in her bed under a mountain of blankets. Her cough had improved, thanks to Alice's special tea, but she couldn't shake the fever and chills. Mustering as much strength as she could manage, she tugged on one of the blankets and pulled it up to her chin. She groaned from the exertion. The weakness that remained in her body was unlike anything she'd ever experienced before.

As close to comfortable as she could get, she rested her head against a stack of pillows and heaved a sigh. She'd tossed and turned all night long, kept awake with a nagging worry—a new premonition on top of the one she'd experienced weeks ago. Whether they were connected, she didn't know.

The queens of ancient times had all had the gift of foresight. Their worries had come with clear visions of troubles to come. But in recent generations, that gift had become diluted. Instead of an actionable prophecy, Patricia had only a sense that something terrible would happen soon. *The curse of the queen's line.*

No specifics. No ability to avoid it—whatever *it* was.

She'd made the right choice to send Jim to a hotel. Of that, she was certain. This virus would have been too much for him. And with an unknown threat looming…at least she knew he was safe. For now.

She heard the creak of a floorboard in the hallway, and her heart skipped a beat. She wasn't alone. "Alice?"

"Coming." Alice bustled into the bedroom carrying a steaming mug of tea. "Oh dear, you look more tired today than yesterday." She set the cup on the nightstand. "Are you feeling worse?"

"I'm just very weak." She started to tell Alice the truth but saw no need to burden her with a queen's worries.

"I'm not surprised. This is a particularly bad strain of the flu from what I hear. And you're still recovering from the binding ritual."

Patricia nodded. She'd been fortunate just to have survived that effort, so a little lingering weakness didn't bother her. It hadn't been much of a problem until she got sick. "I'll be back to my old self in no time." She forced a tight smile.

"Are you sure you don't want me to call Randy?" Alice rested her hand on her plump hip. "He wouldn't mind coming back to help you. You're the queen for goodness' sake."

"No. I don't want to interrupt his vacation for this. I'll be fine." With a grunt, she pushed herself up in her bed. "It's just the flu."

"You're a stubborn queen." Alice fluffed the pillows and waited for her patient to settle in. "Drink up." She placed the tea in Patricia's hand and watched her take a sip. "When you're finished with that, I'll run out and get some supplies for soup. Does chicken noodle sound good?"

Patricia nodded and wrapped her fingers around the mug, warming her hands. When her phone vibrated on the nightstand, she jumped, sloshing hot tea onto her blanket.

"Don't worry. I'll get it for you." Alice glanced at the phone's screen. "It's Stevie."

She gulped and answered the call, hoping it had nothing to do with the sense of dread she had. She listened to her daughter describe Charlie's seizure and took in all of her reassurances that he was safe now.

But if Charlie was safe, why did she still feel so anxious?

Alice took the phone from her after she disconnected the call. "Everything okay?"

"It's time to call Randy. He needs to come home right away." She set her mug of tea on her nightstand. "Charlie is sick now too."

And I want to be prepared for anything.

Chapter nineteen

Stevie

Stevie checked her phone again to see if any messages from Dylan had come in. Nothing. He'd warned her about the cell service at the school, but she didn't think it would be *this* bad. She hadn't heard anything from him since he left. She sighed and tucked her phone back into her pocket. As far as she was concerned, he couldn't get home fast enough.

She glanced at Charlie. He sat upright in the hospital bed, engrossed in a cartoon rerun that played on the wall-mounted television. Awake and alert, he'd suffered no ill effects from his seizure. But she couldn't shake the fear that another one would come.

He flapped his hands, happy with the shenanigans that played out on the television screen. Stevie smiled. She had her boy back.

A willowy young nurse wearing glittery shoes entered the room carrying Charlie's chart. "Good morning. The pediatrician will be in around lunchtime to sign off on Charlie's discharge paperwork."

"Okay, thanks."

The nurse looked up at the ceiling. "I'm so sorry about the lights. It's weird that they aren't working but the television is."

"Yeah, I thought that was odd too. But don't worry about us." Stevie gave a slight wave. "We're fine like this."

Charlie flapped his hands again.

The nurse tucked the chart under her arm. "The electrician is having trouble figuring out what caused them to go out. I'm sure he'll have it fixed soon though."

I bet he won't. Stevie stifled a grin.

She glanced at Charlie and then back at Stevie. "Okay, then. If you need anything, just push the button." She spun around and left the room.

Stevie reached over, taking Charlie's hand in hers. She leaned in close. "Your dad will be here soon. Remember, no magic. Do you understand?"

After several seconds, Charlie nodded, but his gaze never wavered from his favorite cartoon.

"Good." She gave his hand a squeeze before releasing it.

Stevie had just settled back into her seat and gotten swept up in the electronic monotony of children's cartoons when Sam stuck his head inside the doorway. He gave her an awkward wave.

"Hey." She gestured for him to come in.

He slipped into the room and ruffled Charlie's blond locks. "He looks like he's doing better today." He took a seat next to the bed. "Has he said anything else?" Sam raised his eyebrows, a hopeful grin on his face.

She shook her head. "No."

Right now, "magic" was Charlie's only word. And, if everything went well, the odds were slim that Sam would hear him say it again.

Charlie barked a deep, powerful cough. He gasped for air and proceeded to cough even more. Stevie jumped up and rushed to his side. She pressed her hand against his forehead to see if his fever had come back. "No fever."

She passed a plastic cup filled with ice water to her son. Charlie took a sip and then eased back down in his bed.

Stevie pulled the covers over him. "He does pretty good most of the time, but then that cough starts up and wipes him out."

"Stevie." Sam fiddled with the hem of his t-shirt. "I was wondering if it would, um, be okay if I stayed at your place tonight."

Her shoulders stiffened, and she stared at Sam for a long moment. She started to open her mouth to reply but stopped.

Sam leaned forward. "I just want to help with Charlie. I could stay in one of the guest rooms."

Stevie relaxed. "Of course, I'd like that. It would be good to have another set of eyes on him."

Chapter twenty

Patricia

Jarred from her nap, Patricia's eyes flew open at the sound of a creaking floorboard in the hallway.

"Alice?" Her voice was too weak to carry far. Still exhausted, she yawned. She knew she hadn't slept for long.

Hadn't Alice said something about making soup? She waited, listening for a response or the clatter of pots in the kitchen, but she received only silence in reply.

The hairs on the back of her neck stood up. *Something's wrong.* With all her might, she propped herself up into a sitting position. "Alice?" She forced her voice to be louder this time.

Another creak echoed, just outside her bedroom door. "Alice, are you okay?"

Cursing her current state of weakness, she fought against the muscle aches and pushed herself up to stand beside the bed, but she rose too fast. Sharp waves of dizziness assailed her. She gripped the corner of her nightstand to steady herself and forced her body to stand upright. The doorway was only a few feet away, but it might as well have been a mile. She took an uneasy step forward.

A dark blur rushed into the room. Patricia gasped and stumbled back, breathless. She caught a glimpse of a black ski mask and raised her shaky hands in defense. But she was too slow. He stood before her in an instant. She had no time to speak. No time to act.

He thrust something against her shoulder.

A high voltage charge ripped through her entire body. She went rigid, her muscles locked in place as she absorbed the brutal shock.

He yanked the stun gun away from her shoulder. Patricia's rigidness gave way to complete muscle failure. She dropped to the floor with a thud.

Unable to move her head, she lay there, helpless. Drawing in shallow, ragged breaths, she watched his black tasseled loafers creep closer. He bent down and gripped the amulet that hung around her neck. She willed her arms to move, to cover the amethyst that she could no longer hide with her magic. But they wouldn't budge.

The thick gold links jammed into her neck as he tightened his grip on the necklace. With a powerful jerk, he snatched the amulet away from her chest, but its chain held strong. Her attacker tried again with more force. Patricia feared he would snap her neck in the process. She tried to voice her protest, but only a low moan came forth.

His chest heaved with rapid, labored breaths as he shifted the chain until he found the clasp. The necklace trembled in his shaking hands as he struggled to open it.

Paralyzed, Patricia could do nothing to stop him.

The attacker abandoned the clasp and yanked on the necklace once more. This time, he snatched it over Patricia's head. The chain scraped along her scalp as he dragged it between her head and the wooden floor.

No! Patricia's fear gave way to despair as her attacker whipped the necklace away from her motionless body.

He stood over her limp body, the amethyst dangling from his grip. Saying nothing, he spun around and darted out of the room.

His black loafers were the last thing Patricia saw before she lost consciousness.

Chapter twenty-one

Susan

Susan perched on the edge of her bed while she waited for the nurse to leave. She'd tucked her morning medications under her tongue, and the tablets had already begun to dissolve. A bitter taste filled her mouth, but she managed to keep her expression neutral.

Perhaps this will be my last day in the asylum.

As soon as the nurse left, Susan spit the pills into a tissue and tossed them into her trashcan.

Excitement coursed through her veins. In an ideal situation, she would never have collaborated with a religious man. She certainly wouldn't have chosen a descendant of the leader of the Salem witch trial hysteria to work with. But her situation was far from ideal and her options were limited. To his credit, he seemed to despise the coven as much as she did.

The enemy of my enemy.

At least, Chaplain Parris had seen the amulet. He'd managed in a day what others had failed to do for generations—confirm the existence of the powerful amethyst that was nothing more than a legend to some and a long lost artifact to others. That was far more than Vanessa had accomplished. Now Susan knew, without a doubt, that it had survived the centuries on the queens' necks.

This knowledge only added to her resentment of the ruling hierarchy, pouring gasoline on her blazing hatred of the coven. She glanced around her dismal room. Peeling paint. Cracked linoleum. Bars on the window. A vein in her neck throbbed in time with her quickening pulse.

She'd spent countless hours of her twelve-year long imprisonment daydreaming about possessing that amulet. She'd fantasized about its unlimited power and all she could accomplish with it. Now that it was within her grasp, she could not help but consider exactly how she would take down the coven. She balled her hands into fists. No longer would she bow to their authority. In fact, she would demand that they all kneel before her—if she chose to let any of them live.

The sound of a timid knock jarred her from her thoughts. She knew who it was. The corners of her mouth crept upward in a diabolical grin. "Come in, Chaplain."

The door swung open, and Parris entered the drab hospital room. Beads of sweat had formed above his lip and dotted his brow.

"Well?" She arched her eyebrows. "Did you get it?"

He swallowed, averting his gaze. "I had to hurt her." He hung his head.

"But you got the amulet didn't you?" Susan jumped to her feet and threw her hand forward. "Let me see it!"

He didn't look at her. "I'm not sure I have the stomach for this. I thought I could follow in my ancestor's footsteps and lead a modern crusade against witches. Now I'm not so sure. The look in that poor woman's eyes…" His mouth formed a tight line, and he shook his head.

"Poor woman." Susan placed her hands on her hips. "That 'poor woman' is the leader of the witches you seek to destroy. She and her coven are responsible for my imprisonment in this hellhole. There's nothing to pity there." She jabbed his chest. "Now, answer me. Did you get the amulet?"

She pinched her face in disgust at the sight of the trembling man before her. He was too weak, a mere shell of the zealot she'd partnered with. If he couldn't handle having to hurt Patricia in order to retrieve the amulet, she knew he wouldn't stand with her as she executed the rest of her plan.

"Yes, I have the amulet." Parris lifted his head and reached into his pants pocket. Before he withdrew the long awaited prize, he opened his mouth as if to speak but stopped.

Susan licked her lips.

With a defeated sigh, he pulled the amulet and its chain out of his pocket. He gripped the pendant, blocking Susan's view of the amethyst, but the thick gold chain dangled from each side of his closed fist.

Susan gasped, and her eyes widened. She reached forward once again but stopped herself from prying the amulet out of the chaplain's hand. "Please." She swallowed hard. "Give it to me."

"No. I'm sorry. I can't go through with our plan." He clutched the necklace to his chest. "I can't perpetrate violence against these people, no matter how much I disagree with their ways."

Susan held her tongue. She had to be careful, now more than ever. The amethyst was within her grasp, but just out of reach. She could fix that.

"It's quite all right." She strode across the room and closed the door. Once she possessed the amulet, the chaplain would become irrelevant anyway.

"Really, it is." With a saccharine smile, she crept closer to him and rested her hand on top of his tightened fist. "I can put an end to the coven's power all by myself. You won't have to do anything else after you give me that necklace."

Susan sensed the energy from the jewel. Her skin tingled as she listened to a hum in the air only she could hear. She bit down on her lip, stifling a smile. *Soon.*

She dropped her arm to her side and watched as he uncurled his hand, revealing the smooth purple gemstone in all of its glory.

Susan's breath hitched. The amulet would make her whole again. No longer would she be bound to speak only the truth. No longer would she be a prisoner in this hospital.

And never again would she be at the mercy of that wretched coven.

She reached forward, wanting nothing more than to absorb the massive power of the ancient amethyst. Her fingers brushed the gemstone, sending a quake throughout her body.

"No!" Chaplain Parris snapped his fist closed and lurched back from Susan. "I shouldn't have come here. I was upset. I wasn't thinking clearly." He started toward the door.

She couldn't let him go. Not now. Susan's eyes darted around the room in a frantic search for a weapon of any sort. But there was nothing she could use to stop the chaplain. The mirror was unbreakable. There were no lamps or vases. Most of the furniture was nailed down.

Most of it.

The chaplain reached for the door handle.

Her heart raced, thudding with visceral power as adrenaline coursed through her veins. She lunged forward and grabbed the metal chair from the corner of the room. "Chaplain, wait!"

He kept his back to her. "I said no."

Susan swung the chair, slamming it against his head. He fell to the floor, still conscious but dazed. He peered up at her with unfocused eyes and whimpered.

Before he had the opportunity to collect himself, Susan grasped the amulet and yanked it from his hand. Its unfathomable energy pulsed in her palm and flowed up her arm. She slipped the gold chain over her head, allowing the amethyst to fall into place on her chest.

Like a lightning strike, sudden and overwhelming, power flowed through her entire body. What began as a tingling sensation grew to an electric torrent. Thousands of years of history flooded her mind. Secrets and spells known only to the ancestors and descendants of Queen Lucia now waited at her disposal.

Susan drank in the ecstasy of the moment. "I am the queen now!" She threw her head back and laughed.

The chaplain pulled himself up and faced her. Clutching the side of his head, he stared at her in shock. "You said you would stop the practice of witchcraft in Beaufort."

"No, Chaplain." Susan wagged her finger. "I said I would put an end to the coven. And that's a very different thing, isn't it?"

He stepped back, increasing the space between them. "What are you going to do?"

"I'm going to kill that 'poor woman' who used to wear this lovely necklace." She stepped toward the stainless steel mirror and studied her own reflection. "There can only be one queen, you know."

She whipped her head around and sneered at Parris. "You *should* be asking what I'm going to do with you. You've already told me you don't have the stomach to go through with our witch hunt. That makes you useless to me." She patted the amulet. It was everything she needed.

His eyes bulged, and his mouth fell open. "But I…" He twisted away from her and grasped for the door handle. An unseen force stopped him.

Susan cackled. She'd blocked his escape with little more than a thought. With another burst of concentrated power, she spun him around to face her.

He raised his hands and squeezed his eyes shut. "Please don't hurt me."

Susan stalked closer to him, beginning another magical endeavor made possible by the amulet. Electric energy roiled within her, tingling her fingertips and churning her stomach.

"Look at me!" What she intended to do would be magnificent to watch, and she didn't want him to miss a minute of it. Fueled by his whimpers, she began her transformation.

She watched the color drain from his face as she grew three inches taller. Her long, graying hair turned brown and shrank back, cropping itself into a style resembling his. Her cheekbones morphed, her bones shifted, and her wrinkles disappeared until she was a mirror image of Parris. Her velour lounge suit changed into a shirt, tie, and dress pants.

She'd become an identical copy of the chaplain, even down to his black tasseled loafers.

He recoiled in horror. "You…you look just like me."

"Not for long." Susan spoke like him, complete with his Massachusetts accent. She'd duplicated his voice as precisely as she'd copied his appearance.

With nothing more than a wave of her arm, the chaplain began his transformation. In an instant, he morphed into Susan's image—lounge suit and all.

"No. Don't do this!" He clapped his hand over his mouth as his new feminine voice rang out.

"I wouldn't bother telling anyone about this. No one would believe you." She winked as she threw his own words back at him. "The nurse will come around with your medications in a few hours. Take them. That'll make the adjustment a little easier for you."

"Change me back! You can't leave me like this!" The chaplain's voice rose to a shriek.

"Shhh." Susan pressed her finger to her lips. "They don't like screaming around here. You get extra medicine if you do that." She hunched forward and smirked. "The kind that comes in a *needle*."

Her warning did nothing to calm the chaplain. He continued to scream in her voice.

The door flew open, and a nurse, along with two orderlies, barged in. Alarmed, the nurse looked to the Susan-turned-chaplain. She pointed to the terrified woman. "What's going on in here? Why is she screaming like that?"

Susan shrugged. "I have no idea. She just kind of snapped. You should probably give her the good stuff." She walked out of the room without glancing back.

Still wearing a magical version of the chaplain's face, Susan made her way down the hall to the desk closest to the exit. While she waited for the nurse on duty to buzz the security door open, she remembered a promise she'd made to Doctor Max a few weeks earlier. She had no intention of ever returning to this horrible place, so she'd have to handle the matter now.

119

"Excuse me. Is Doctor Max in his office?"

The young woman behind the counter shook her head. "No. He has the flu. He'll be out for the rest of the week." She pressed the button to unlock the door and a buzzer sounded.

"Lucky guy." Susan passed through the door, leaving the misery of the hospital behind her.

Chapter twenty-two

Patricia

Patricia's eyes fluttered open as she lay on the cool, wooden floor of her bedroom. Every muscle in her body ached. Blurred images flashed in her memory—a dark figure, a ski mask, the amulet.

"The amulet!" She struggled to pull herself up, managing only to reach a sitting position. She looked down at her chest and patted it in search of the pendant. Her duty had been to protect it. And she'd failed.

"It's gone." Never before in the thousands of years of her ancestors' history had a reigning queen lost the amulet.

Never.

The front door creaked open, and her breath caught in her throat. *He's back!* She opened her hands, willing her magic to pool within her palms. She knew the odds of defeating a witch armed with the amulet were nonexistent. But she also knew that she was willing to die in order to retrieve it.

Unable to stand, she propped herself against the side of her bed and drove her hands forward, aiming toward the doorway. She waited, body tensed, and listened to the heavy footsteps creep closer to her bedroom. Another floorboard creaked. She was ready to strike as soon as he entered the room.

Floral fabric swished in the doorway. *Alice.*

Patricia's shoulders slumped. It wasn't him. She closed her fists, squelching her magic.

Alice dropped her bags and rushed to Patricia's side. "Oh my goodness! What happened?" She offered her hand to help Patricia stand up. "Did you fall? You shouldn't have been out of bed. You need your rest."

Finally standing and exhausted from the effort, Patricia struggled to catch her breath and steadied herself. She placed a hand on Alice's shoulder and met the old witch's worried gaze. "Alice, someone broke into my house while you were out."

"Oh no! Were you hurt?" Alice studied Patricia, searching for any sign of bodily harm. "Were you attacked?"

Patricia's eyes glistened with unshed tears. "We all were, Alice."

Alice crinkled her forehead. "What do you mean?"

"Our entire coven, all of the Beaufort witches." She pressed her hand against her chest. "We are *all* under attack."

"I don't understand."

"The amulet was stolen." Patricia's voice cracked. "I've failed you all."

She hung her head in shame.

Chapter twenty-three

Vanessa

From the discomfort of her hospital bed, Vanessa flipped through the limited channel selection offered by the small television. Throughout the morning, her thoughts kept returning to Charlie and his middle-of-the-night visit. She knew little about the boy, but she'd sensed his forgiveness for her previous attempt on his life.

Forgiveness. It was a foreign concept to Vanessa. Susan had raised her on a hearty diet of rage and revenge. In their world of dark magic, to forgive meant to allow continued wrongdoings or to condone perceived slights. It was a sign of weakness, one that the Moore women would not indulge under any circumstance.

With a sigh, she sank back against the pillow. She didn't like children, but there was something about Charlie that had affected her. He was different from other kids she'd encountered. It was something apart from his powerful magic, a quality that resonated throughout his whole being. She shook her head, puzzled by her unexpected regard for him.

Voices in the hallway snapped her out of her ruminations. She muted the television so she could listen in, hoping to catch some information regarding the boy. She had no idea why Charlie was staying in the hospital or how long he would be there, but Vanessa knew her life was in danger while his mother was close by. The sooner he left, the better.

The chatter in the hall turned out to be nothing more than two nurses discussing the flu epidemic and the hospital's inevitable march to full capacity. Vanessa bit her lip. She would have to leave soon, and she still hadn't figured out where to go. She'd left her yacht docked in Beaufort, but she wouldn't be safe there. If she returned, the members of the coven would soon discover her presence. Perhaps she could find a nice oceanfront hotel in Atlantic Beach with room service. *It would sure beat this place.*

A man's voice, unfamiliar to her, interrupted the nurses' conversation in the hallway. "I was told Vanessa Moore is on this floor. Which room is hers?"

She wasn't expecting anyone. She kept watch on her door as she sat up, waiting for the strange man to enter. Footsteps drew closer until a shadow loomed in her doorway. The man entered her room, closing the heavy door behind him. Without a word, he crossed the small space until he reached the window. Vanessa expected him to introduce himself, but instead, he studied the view outside as if he'd never seen a sunny day before.

Vanessa crossed her arms. "Who are you?"

The man twirled around to face her, his grin full of unexplained exuberance. The corners of his mouth dipped down and his nose crinkled in revulsion as his gaze fell upon her scarred face.

He stepped closer to get a better look at her scars. "You are hideous!"

Vanessa recoiled from the comment and raised a hand to her face, covering her monstrous burns. No one had said anything so hurtful since her accident. The medical professionals who'd treated her had hidden their disgust well.

No matter how she looked, she wasn't going to let anyone talk to her like that. Heat flushed through her body, and she dropped her hand to her lap. "I don't know who the hell you are, and I don't care. Just get out of here!" She jerked her arm forward and pointed to the door.

The man raised his hands as if to calm a large crowd. "Wait a minute." He cleared his throat. "Let me try this again." He thought for a moment. "Your burns aren't so bad. I'm sure no one will even notice them."

Vanessa glared at the bizarre man whose chilling grin grew larger.

"Ha! I did it!" He slapped his knee in triumph as he threw his head back and laughed. "I lied! I told a lie. The spell is broken."

The spell is broken. Her jaw fell slack, and her heart began to race. It couldn't be. "Who are you?"

Vanessa shook her head in disbelief as the stranger transformed in front of her. His brown hair sprouted into long, gray tendrils. The man's height diminished, and his frame thinned while his dress slacks and shirt turned into a black, gauzy dress. His cheekbones plumped, morphing into the familiar feminine face of Susan.

Vanessa lurched forward, shocked. "Mother!"

"More important than that." Susan showed no interest in a poignant mother-daughter reunion. Instead, she cradled the large amethyst pendant in her hand. "I am the queen!"

In a million years, Vanessa never would have expected to see her mother outside of the psychiatric hospital. Not like this anyway. Certainly not armed with the amulet. Countless questions darted through her mind.

"It's time to get to work. I'll fill you in on all the details later." Susan released the amethyst and let it fall onto her chest. She stepped back toward the window, once again taking in the sights of the street below. "Are you still having the coven members watched by a private investigator? I need to know everything about them. I have big plans."

Vanessa opened her mouth to speak, but words failed her. She could only stare at her mother.

"Answer me!" Susan whipped around and glared at her. "I didn't come here to waste time!"

A lump formed in Vanessa's throat. Her mother hadn't come to visit out of any interest in her well-being. She merely wanted access to Vanessa's resources, and it seemed she wanted a witness to whatever horrors she had planned for the coven.

"Yes, they are still being tracked." She curled her fingers around the edge of her blanket. "But I haven't checked in with the detective in a while. I really couldn't tell you what's going on with those people at this point."

"Then we need to find out." Susan gestured for her follow. "Come on now. Let's go." She began to walk toward the door.

"I don't have any clothes here." Vanessa glanced down at her thin hospital gown. The clothing she'd had on when she arrived had been tattered and burned in the explosion. She couldn't leave like this.

Susan sighed and flicked her wrist. In an instant, Vanessa found herself wearing a loose-fitting sweatshirt and matching fleece pants. She cringed. The outfit was only a little better than wearing the open-backed hospital gown out in public.

"It has a hood. So you can hide your atrocious face. No one wants to see that." She gestured for Vanessa to hurry. "Well, go ahead. Pull up that hood."

"Yes, Mother." She slipped the hood over her head and then forced herself to stand. The new skin that had begun to form over her wounds tugged with every movement. She winced in pain.

Maybe Mother will help me.

Susan stood by the door, tapping her foot. "Hurry up."

She shuffled to her mother's side. "Wait." She cracked the door open just enough to see down the hall. No nurses or doctors milled about, so she motioned for Susan to follow her. "Okay, let's go."

Irritated, Susan snatched the door open. "We have nothing to fear now, Vanessa. I have the amulet. We are protected."

She peeked under the edge of her hood, watching for any signs of movement in front of them. Walking as fast as she could force herself to move, she shifted her body away from each open door as they continued down the long hall. She wanted to get out of the hospital without being spotted by Charlie or any of his family members.

Vanessa knew no one could hurt her now that Susan had the amulet—but it wasn't her own safety she was concerned with.

chapter twenty-four

Stevie

After the doctor signed the dismissal papers, Sam drove them home in his old pickup truck. Stevie watched Charlie sleep in his car seat and ran through the list of discharge instructions in her mind. Rest. Fluids. Keep the fever down. Come back to the hospital if he has another seizure.

Another seizure. Stevie closed her eyes, the first one still lingered in her memory. She couldn't bear the thought of another one.

When they crossed the bridge into Beaufort, she glanced out the window. *Home.* She'd only been away for a night, but it had seemed so much longer. She took comfort in the familiar landmarks of her little town, sighing as they passed long stretches of cozy cottages with historic plaques displayed by their front doors.

A double-decker tour bus, with a handful of tourists on board, traveled ahead of them. Stevie remembered taking that tour in middle school. She knew those passengers were hearing all about the activities of pirates and confederate spies in the old days of Beaufort. *But they'll never hear the full history of this place.* They wouldn't learn about the three women who sank

Blackbeard's ship in 1718, nor would they ever learn of the generations of witches who'd lived in the town for the last three centuries.

They turned right onto Front Street and drove past the Maritime Museum, as well as several grand old houses that faced the serene water of Taylor's Creek. Like Stevie's home, they were well-preserved historic residences that harkened back to simpler times.

Sam parked his truck on the street in front of Stevie's house. Charlie stirred and woke as his father lifted him from the car seat and carried him up the walkway to the porch.

Stevie unlocked the door and pushed it open. "Let's put him in the den."

"You got it." Sam carried Charlie through the house and placed him on the couch.

They worked in tandem, like they'd done when Charlie was younger. She didn't have to ask Sam for anything, he just did what was needed. Stevie covered their son with a blanket while Sam went to the kitchen to get him a glass of water. She prepared the next dose of fever-reducing medication, and he clicked on the television, setting it to a cartoon channel.

Glad for his help, Stevie gave Sam a grateful smile.

By the time they were finished, Charlie had everything he needed to rest in comfort on the couch. Stevie placed the iPad by his side in case he needed it to communicate or play. The medicine controlled his fever well, but both she and Sam remained nearby, ever watchful.

Stevie found her phone on the floor, where it had fallen during Charlie's seizure. An image of his oxygen-deprived body flashed in her mind. A wave of nausea washed through her at the memory, and her heart began to pound as though it were all happening again. She wiped the dampness from her brow. The flashbacks were almost as awful as the real thing.

In an effort to distract herself from the unwanted memory, she checked her phone for messages. Much to her disappointment, she'd still received no word from Dylan. Her shoulders slumped.

"Is something wrong?" Sam gave her a quizzical glance.

"It's just, uh…" She slipped the phone into her pocket. "It's nothing."

Stevie heard the sound of a car pull up in front of her house. "Someone's here." She started toward the hallway.

"How do you know that?"

With her back to Sam, she grimaced. He couldn't have heard the car like she had. She pretended not to hear his question and made her way to the front of the house. She glanced through the window and saw Randy's champagne colored Buick.

Ever the gentleman, Randy let himself out of the car and then walked around to the passenger side to open the door for Ruth.

Stevie stepped onto her porch to greet them, curious about the perfect timing of their visit.

"Do you know what happened to Charlie?" She leaned in close and kept her voice low. "Did you have a vision?"

"Actually, Alice called me this morning and told me what happened." Randy slipped his keys into his pocket. "I…uh… didn't have any visions while we were away."

Ruth snorted. "That's because I didn't let him get much sleep."

Stevie glanced between the two very senior members of the coven as she realized what Ruth meant. A painful silence fell between them.

Randy cleared his throat. "How's he doing?" He nodded toward Stevie's house.

"He's resting. Sam's in there with him now." She exhaled, relieved by the change of topic. "We'll have to get him out of the room so you can heal Charlie."

"Not necessary. I can be very discreet." Randy waved away Stevie's concerns. His blue eyes twinkled as he smiled at her. "Remember when we visited your father in the emergency room after his heart attack?"

At the time, she'd thought nothing of Randy's visit to her dad's bedside. She didn't recall anything unusual about his presence. But she did remember the surprise of the attending physician when he discovered that Jim's massive attack had caused no damage to his heart muscle.

Stevie grinned and gestured for them to follow. "Come on inside."

Ruth and Randy followed Stevie into the house, and she led them to Charlie. Sam greeted them with a friendly nod.

"Sam, Randy's going to take a look at Charlie for me. He may be retired, but he'll always be our family doctor."

"Sure, go ahead, Doc." Sam stepped away from Charlie to make room for the doctor. "Didn't know there was anyone around still making house calls. Where's your bag?"

"Oh right. I think I left it by the door." He glanced at Ruth. "Would you mind?"

Stevie knew that the doctor had not come in with his black bag, but she wasn't the least bit surprised when Ruth returned to the den and handed it to Randy. She wondered how often, in this small town full of witches, secret magic had been performed in the presence of the uninitiated.

Randy removed his stethoscope from his bag and listened to Charlie's chest. He nodded. "His immune system is strong, and this appears to be a relatively mild case of the flu. I wouldn't be at all surprised if he took a long nap and woke up feeling much better." He winked at Stevie.

"That sounds about right. He probably gets his immune system from me." Sam patted his chest. "I never get sick."

Stevie resisted the urge to giggle. If Randy intended to prepare Sam for Charlie's speedy recovery, it was working perfectly.

Randy rested his hand on Charlie's forehead. "His fever is under control, so his risk of having another seizure is very low." Randy met Stevie's gaze and smiled.

Stevie relaxed. The doctor's grin told her everything she needed to know. Charlie was safe.

"Thanks for letting me examine you. You were a very good boy." Randy patted Charlie's head and spoke in a deep, soothing voice. "Go to sleep now. You'll feel better soon."

The corners of Charlie's mouth turned up in a slight smile and his eyelids grew heavy.

As he drifted off to sleep, he whispered, "Magic."

"It's the darnedest thing. That's what he said when he woke up in the hospital too." Sam beamed. "Strange thing to say. But as long as he's talking, I'm not going to complain about his choice of words."

Ruth and Randy exchanged a glance but said nothing.

"I need to go check on your mom now, Stevie. I understand that her case of the flu is particularly bad." Randy snapped his bag closed. "I would have checked on her first, but she said she wouldn't see me until after I examined Charlie."

"That sounds just like Mom." Stevie snickered. "Can I ride along with you? Since Charlie's sleeping, it's a good time for me to stop by and see her." Stevie turned to Sam. "Do you mind hanging out here while I go?"

"Not at all. I told you, I'm here for the duration." Sam shooed her out the door.

Stevie followed Ruth and Randy outside to the old Buick. "Thanks so much for coming to help Charlie." Stevie squinted in the bright sun. "But I'm really sorry that your trip got cut short. Were you able to visit some of the lighthouses at least before you had to come back?"

Randy paused before answering. "Not this time." He grabbed Ruth's hand and gave it a gentle kiss before opening the car door for her.

Ruth cast Stevie a sideways glance. "He did get to see me though." She cackled as she eased into the passenger seat of the Buick. "He saw a whole lot of me."

Randy's cheeks grew bright red. He kept his head down as he opened the back door of the car for Stevie. No one spoke during the short drive to Patricia's house.

Chapter twenty-five

Vanessa

Vanessa listened to Susan's detailed story of her escape from the psychiatric hospital as they drove to the Beaufort waterfront in a stolen Lexus. She "oohed" and "ah-hed" at all the right times, making sure to give Susan the accolades she knew her mother expected.

When Susan finally finished her boastful tale, her tone changed. "You should feel very foolish right now." She wagged her finger. "A man, just a regular man, was able to acquire the amulet for me. A task you failed miserably."

Vanessa stared out the window as they crossed the bridge into Beaufort, over the body of water in which Dylan's mother had perished twelve years earlier. She remembered standing beside Susan while she used her magic to toss Rebecca Kent's car into the water. She'd never asked why, never expressed her concerns about the murder of a fellow witch. As a teenager, she'd followed Susan's cruel plan to destroy the coven as if it were the only plausible course of action. She'd never considered that there might be another path to take. If she had known then what she knew now, would she have followed so blindly?

It didn't matter. Even as a grown woman, she remained under her mother's control. Now that Susan had the amulet, Vanessa was dependent on her to reinstate her magical gifts.

"Mother, I sacrificed everything trying to get that amulet for you." Vanessa regretted the words as soon as they left her lips. She shrank back beneath her hood.

"Oh did you? Well, you clearly you didn't try hard enough." Susan sneered. "You disgust me. It's a wonder I even came to get you at all."

"Why did you come for me?" Vanessa crossed her arms and cast a sidelong glance at her mother. But she already knew the answer. Susan had never loved her. Bloodlust and revenge always came first.

"Because you can be of service to me. Perhaps you can redeem yourself." She paused for a moment. "If you can manage to help without screwing everything up, of course."

They rode in silence for a short while longer until the docks on Front Street came into view. Amid the array of yachts and sailboats, Vanessa spotted her own sleek vessel. "There it is." She directed her mother to park in the public lot on the waterfront.

After abandoning the car in the parking area, they made their way onto the deck of the yacht. Vanessa stole a quick glance down Front Street and shivered. Stevie's house was only a few blocks away. She didn't want to be here, but her mother had refused to settle for anything else.

It wouldn't be long before the coven noticed she was back—unless Susan got to them first.

She followed Susan into the cabin and watched her mother take in its modern decor. The older witch ran her hands along the polished wood countertops. Then she stroked the fine leather of the built-in couch, which faced a large flat screen television.

"This is how you lived while I wasted away in the mental institution?" Susan spun around to glare at her daughter.

"Mother, I offered to get you out of there. More than once. You turned me down because the coven would have come after you, remember?" Vanessa lowered her gaze. "I...I tried to help you."

Susan did not reply. Instead, she grabbed the phone from the end table and shoved it in Vanessa's face. "Here. Call your investigator. I need to know everything about that coven."

Already exhausted, Vanessa took the phone and settled in on the couch. She dialed his number, noting that he answered her call on the first ring. Given what she paid him for his services, she would expect nothing less. She asked for an update on the Beaufort Historic Society members, skipping any pleasantries.

In the years that the investigator had worked for her, he'd never once asked why she wanted them tracked. Maybe he was accustomed to bizarre requests. Maybe he was just being professional. Whatever the case, he was reliably discreet, and Vanessa appreciated that. She listened as he filled her in on his latest observations, current as of the day before.

Susan stared at Vanessa once the call ended. "Well?"

"Randy, Ruth, and Dylan are all out of town."

"Together?" Susan narrowed her eyes.

Vanessa shook her head. "Dylan left first. He flew out of the Beaufort airfield on his private jet. He may have gone back to London, but my investigator couldn't say for sure. Ruth and Randy left together by car."

"Well, when are they coming back?" Susan threw her hands up in the air.

"He didn't say." Vanessa traced the edge of her phone with her finger. "He has no way of knowing that."

Susan began to pace the length of the cabin. "What about the others? What's going on with them?"

The investigator had also shared something that Vanessa already knew—that Charlie was in the hospital and Stevie was there with him. Her stomach clenched. "Nothing. That was it."

"It's not very helpful." Susan's stopped pacing and put her hands on her hips. "What about special gifts? Do you know anything about what the coven members can do?"

Again, Vanessa shook her head. Most witches kept their special gifts a secret. If any of the coven members had a unique talent, they'd never reveal it.

"Hmmm." Susan stroked the amethyst pendant. "Perhaps I can get more information from the amulet. It's already shown me so much, so it's probably just a matter of time before it reveals the secrets of the coven members."

Vanessa wondered what her role would be in the coven's downfall. She couldn't imagine how useful she would be in her weakened state. The amulet had restored Susan's powers. Perhaps it would do the same for her.

She swallowed hard and forced herself to face her mother. "I need my magic back."

"It's easier to regain power than it is to take it away. The coven probably used an old-fashioned ritual to bind your magic. Maybe if you asked very nicely, one of them would give it back to you." She cackled at her own joke.

"That will never happen." Vanessa pursed her lips, disgusted by her mother's heartlessness. "I thought you could help me."

"My powers came back when I placed the amethyst around my neck. I imagine that would work for you too, but then I'd have to let *you* wear *my* amulet." She punctuated her statement by pointing to Vanessa and then herself. "How could I be certain that you'd give it back to me?"

How could her mother ask that? After all the sacrifices she'd made? She watched Susan stroke the purple gemstone with more affection than she'd ever shown her. Vanessa clenched her jaw.

"What about my burns? With your gift restored, you can disguise them for me." She didn't want to walk around town in her gruesome state. Susan was no healer, but Vanessa knew that she was more than capable of at least concealing the damage done in the explosion.

"Perhaps I will hide the scars for you someday. But not yet." Susan clucked. "Consider this your punishment. You have to learn your lesson."

Vanessa looked away from her mother and let her gaze fall to the floor. She had already learned a valuable lesson, but it surely wasn't the one Susan wanted her to learn.

Chapter twenty-six

Stevie

Stevie arrived to find her mother pale and tired, lying on her couch covered in a heap of blankets. Randy rushed to Patricia's side and began the process of healing her of the flu virus. Ruth stood in the doorway with a rare gleam in her eye, watching him work his powerful magic.

Alice hovered beside the couch, just as pale and shaken as Patricia.

Concerned, Stevie wrinkled her brow. "Alice, are you sick too?"

"Me? No, dear. I'm okay." Alice wrung her hands. Her worried gaze never wavered from Patricia.

"Mom will be fine." Stevie patted her shoulder. "Randy will have her feeling better in no time. He just did the same for Charlie."

Alice frowned. "Randy can't fix——"

"Not now, Alice." Patricia coughed. "Wait for the others."

Stevie glanced between the two women, alarmed. "What's going on?"

Alice shook her head as tears welled in her eyes. She began to pace across the living room.

Randy finished healing Patricia and helped her sit upright. Color had returned to her face, and she pushed her blankets off. "Thank you, Randy." She glanced down at her long, flannel nightgown. "I'll be back in a minute. I just need to get dressed."

Stevie heard the front door swing open. She peered down the hallway and spotted Lexi and Deborah walking toward the den.

"We're here." Lexi wrapped an arm around Stevie. "How's Charlie?"

"He's good. Randy took care of him." Stevie tilted her head. "Why are you here?"

"Alice called and told us to come over right away." She raised her chin in the senior witch's direction. "She said it was urgent. What's going on?"

All of the witches looked to Alice for an explanation.

Her knuckles grew redder from her fervent hand wringing. "You should all probably sit down."

Stevie had never seen Alice so distraught before. She couldn't bring herself to sit down. Locked in a whirlwind of fret and uncertainty, she knew something was very wrong. She cast a worried glance at Lexi, whose furrowed brow echoed her own concerns. No one uttered a word.

Ruth inched closer to Randy and grabbed his hand.

With heavy steps, Patricia returned to the den. She'd brushed her hair and changed into an ankle length, navy blue dress with a batik design along the hem. Though all signs of her illness had vanished, her deep frown remained. "Yes, please. Everyone take a seat." She gestured toward the couch and chairs. "You too, Alice. You look like you might faint."

Alice nodded and followed Patricia's direction, as did everyone else. They waited in silence for their queen to speak. Stevie wiped her palms on her jeans, studying the pained expression on her mother's face and dreading whatever she was about to say.

Patricia drew in a deep breath. "The amulet has been stolen."

The queen's words crashed through the stillness of the room. Stevie's mouth fell open, and her shoulders hunched forward as though she'd taken a punch to her stomach. She braced her hands against her knees, steeling herself for more.

"I have no idea who took the amulet, but I'm certain it was a man." Patricia filled in the coven members on the events of the morning. Sparing no detail, she told them everything she could remember, up to and including the man's black tasseled loafers.

Alice shook her head. "I just can't imagine who would do such a thing. All of our threats..." She paused and glanced at Stevie. "Have been eliminated."

Lexi pulled her hand away from her mouth. "No one outside of this coven has even *seen* the amulet."

"That's true, but the man who was in here this morning knew about it. He didn't bother to search for money or other jewelry; he went straight for the amethyst." Patricia touched her neck, as if she hoped to find the lost pendant there. "Even Vanessa was never so bold in her quest to take it."

The mention of Vanessa's name sent a shiver down Stevie's spine. "Only because she didn't know that you wore it."

"Wait a minute." Alice held a finger up. "There was one person who might have seen the amulet. But he couldn't possibly be..." She lowered her hand and shook her head.

Patricia nodded, remembering. "There was a chaplain who stopped by while I was sick. It's possible that the amulet became visible while I was coughing. I was so weak then; I didn't even realize…"

"Who is this chaplain?" Ruth crossed her arms.

"He's a very nice man. Well, that was my impression anyway." Alice's white eyebrows drew together. "I even invited him to deliver the sermon at our church on Sunday. His name is Benjamin Parris."

Patricia groaned. "I knew his name was familiar. I was just too sick to put it together at the time."

Anxious for more information, Stevie's gaze darted from Alice to Patricia. She'd never heard of this man before.

"Parris?" Deborah arched her eyebrows. "Could he be a descendant of Samuel Parris?"

"I suppose he could be. But it didn't occur to me that there might be a connection. It's been so long since those dark days." Alice's cheeks flushed, and she dropped her head. "I just didn't think to ask."

Stevie straightened her back. "I don't understand. Who is Samuel Parris?"

Lexi faced her with a grim expression. "He was the Puritan minister behind the Salem witch trials in 1692."

Stevie's heart sank. This could not be a coincidence.

Crimson patches stretched across Ruth's cheeks as she balled her hands into fists. "Unbelievable! This man will start up the witch hunts all over again. Right here in Beaufort."

"Calm down, Ruth." Patricia held her hand up. "We don't know what his intentions are. I can't even say for sure that it was the chaplain who attacked me."

142

Randy cleared his throat. "He seems to be our most likely suspect right now."

"I don't think this man is a witch." Patricia shook her head. "He used no magic against me."

"Then it should be easy enough to retrieve it from him." Deborah offered an encouraging smile.

Stevie wasn't convinced that anything about this would be easy. That man had attacked her mother and stolen the amulet. *There's no telling what else he's capable of.* As her stomach twisted in an uneasy knot, she rose from her seat on the couch and left the room. *We need Dylan.*

I need Dylan.

She pulled her phone from her back pocket and dialed his number. The call went straight to his voicemail. *Still no cell service.* She tightened her grip on the phone and left him a message.

"Please call as soon as possible. It's urgent. Come home if you can—as soon as you can." She wanted to say more, but she held back. "We need you." She disconnected the call and slipped the phone back into her pocket. She knew he'd come back to help *if* he got her message.

Chapter twenty-seven

Vanessa

Vanessa stood alone on the deck of her yacht. She'd hidden her scarred face as much as she could with her hood, but she still avoided turning toward the people who walked along the docks. Wincing, she envisioned them recoiling in horror at the sight of the full scope of her burns. *I'm not prepared to deal with that yet.*

She stared down at the calm water below. Its glassy surface reflected the brilliant shades of red and orange provided by the fall sunset blazing in the sky above.

A child's giggles echoed across Taylor's Creek, and Vanessa heard the patter of his small feet running along the wooden docks. She imagined the boy's parents trailing behind him, hand in hand, smiling in the light of their child's glee.

They have no idea of the danger in their midst.

Vanessa sighed. That family enjoyed a life she would never know. She'd always been on her own, and now, her burns ensured that she would stay that way. The thought left her with an unexpected tightness in her chest.

I'll always be like this. Hideous. Powerless. Alone.

She closed her eyes, remembering the sensation of the wind in her long hair and the kiss of the cool breeze along the once smooth skin of her cheek. She thought of her countless skimpy dresses and the thrill she'd enjoyed knowing that all eyes were on her when she wore them. Those days were over now.

Unless she could somehow earn her mother's approval.

Susan returned to the yacht as the last light of day faded from the sky. "I disposed of our *borrowed* car. So there's no need to worry about that—not that the police could do anything to us anyway." She laughed and took a seat on one of the upholstered deck chairs.

Vanessa, more comfortable under the cover of darkness, twisted around to glimpse at her mother. She kept her head low so that her hood draped over her cheeks.

"Are you ready to hear my plan?" Susan beamed with pride.

Vanessa bit her lip. She couldn't deny that she was curious, but she had a remarkable lack of enthusiasm. Participating in Susan's embittered revenge plots had never served her well, but her desire to please her mother superseded her instinct to run from the coven. She raised her hand to her face, touching a lumpy stretch of scars along her cheek. If she could make her mother happy, she might be able to regain her powers and hide her burns. *I have nothing left to lose anyway.*

She sighed, releasing her remaining uncertainty. "Sure."

Susan's eyes lit up as she laid out a flawless plan of fear, confusion, and pain that would lead to the ultimate destruction of the coven. Devastation was certain and death guaranteed.

Vanessa hid beneath her hood and swallowed hard. A few weeks earlier, she might have reveled in her mother's cleverness. She might have even added her own stamp of fiendishness to the scheme. But not this time. Not after the suffering she had endured. Not after her time with Charlie in the hospital.

"Why go to so much trouble, Mother?" Vanessa tilted her head. "You have the amulet now. We could leave this town and go anywhere in the world."

Susan sneered and rose from her chair. She jammed her finger in Vanessa's chest. "How can you even ask such a question? After what they did to me! To us!" She lowered her hand and turned away. "I didn't think it was possible for you to be any more of a disappointment."

"I'm thinking of the boy. He's just a kid." *He doesn't deserve this.*

Susan threw her head back and laughed. "Kids can turn on you."

All of a sudden, a helicopter roared overhead and shone a spotlight down on Vanessa. The wind from its spinning blades blew her hood back, exposing the scars on her face and scalp. Her few remaining patches of long hair flapped in the relentless gusts. Before she had a chance to escape the blinding light, a gaggle of small children surrounded her on the deck. Some screamed in horror at the sight of her face; others pointed and laughed.

"Monster!" They shouted in unison. "She's a monster!"

She twisted, eyes darting in every direction, desperately seeking a way to escape the children, but the terrifying mob encircled her. The children crept closer as their shrieks intensified, pelting her with loathing and revulsion. The heat from the light above burned the delicate new skin on her scars.

"No! Leave me alone!"

They ignored her pleas. One grabbed her burned hand and squeezed down on the tender flesh. Vanessa howled and jumped back, only to watch them squeal in delight of her agony. They closed in on her, shouting, poking, cackling. The cacophony of their unrelenting hate grew louder and louder until she could endure it no more. She clasped her hands over her ears and squeezed her eyes shut. "Stop it!"

Silence. She opened her eyes and lowered her hands. There were no children on the deck, no helicopter overhead. There never had been.

She was safely ensconced in the darkness once more. She pulled her hood back up, taking care to cover the left side of her face. Drawing in ragged breaths, she stared at her mother. Despair gave way to anger, and she clenched her teeth.

Susan wore a thin grin as she stepped toward the cabin door. "I believe I've made my point."

Chapter twenty-eight

Stevie

When Stevie returned home, she found Sam and Charlie in the kitchen.

Sam loaded a plate in the dishwasher. "He must be on the mend. He ate all of his dinner and some of mine too." He cocked his head toward the table where Charlie sat. "He didn't cough at all while you were gone either."

Stevie pressed her hand to Charlie's forehead. No fever. She closed her eyes, relieved. Randy's magic had worked. At least she didn't have to worry about the flu on top of the missing amulet.

"Thanks for fixing dinner." She forced a thin smile. "I didn't mean to be gone as long as I was."

Sam looked up from the sink and his eyes grew wide. "Geez, Stevie. Are you okay? I hope you're not getting sick too." He stepped toward her and placed a hand on her forehead. "No fever, but you look rough." He let his hand fall to his side. "Maybe you should get some rest. I can take care of Charlie."

Stevie shook her head and dismissed his concern with a wave. "I'm okay. Just worried about my mom."

"She's got it pretty bad, huh?" Sam returned to the sink and finished scrubbing a pan.

It's so much worse than that. "Yeah."

"Are you hungry? I fixed a plate for you too." He dried his hands on a towel. "It's in the fridge."

"Thanks, but I don't have much of an appetite right now. Maybe later."

"Okay. It's there for you when you're ready." Sam glanced at his watch and then turned to Charlie. "I think we have time to catch a cartoon before bedtime. What do you think?"

Charlie jumped up from his chair and scooted out of the room.

Stevie chuckled. "I guess we know what he thinks of that plan."

They followed Charlie to the den and joined him on the couch, each taking a seat on either side of him. Stevie settled in next to her son and watched all the colorful characters parade across the television screen.

Though she knew Charlie was fine, she didn't ask Sam to leave. As far as he knew, their son was still at risk of having another seizure, and she couldn't tell him otherwise.

Before long, she and Sam were laughing together at the silly antics playing out before them, just like they used to do. Reveling in the easy comfort of their family time, the tension in Stevie's shoulders let go.

As the show came to an end, Stevie patted Charlie's knee. "It's time for bed." She took his hand in hers and together they climbed the stairs.

Stevie selected his favorite dinosaur pajamas from his dresser and helped him change into them. He jumped into his bed with far more exuberance than anyone suffering from the flu should have been able to do. As soon as he rested his head on the pillow, Stevie ruffled his blond curls and planted a kiss on his forehead. "I love you."

She spun around to leave the room and spotted Sam leaning against the doorway. "Oh!" She clapped her hand against her chest. "I didn't know you were there."

"Sorry. I didn't mean to scare you." He straightened up, smiling his crooked grin. "I just miss this." He walked over to Charlie and kissed him on the top of his head. "Good night."

Stevie bit her lip. She missed it too.

As they stepped out into the hallway together, Sam yawned. "I'm beat. I think I'll head to bed too." He made his way toward one of the guest rooms.

"Yeah, it's been a long day." Stevie padded across the hall to her own bedroom but stopped just outside the doorway. "Sam?"

He glanced back at her, eyebrows raised. "Yeah?"

"Thanks."

He gave a deep nod. "Anytime."

Between Charlie's seizure, the hospital stay, and the news of Patricia's attack, Stevie's body ached with exhaustion. She slipped into a tank top and shorts and climbed into her bed. Pulling the covers up to her chin, she sank back against her pillow.

She closed her eyes, expecting sleep to come soon. But in the stillness of the night, flashes of unwanted memories came back to haunt her. Blue skin. Vacant stare. She tossed and turned, trying to shake the unbidden images away. They terrified her as much as Charlie's seizure had.

He's fine. Randy healed him.

She managed to doze off, only to slip back into the nightmare of the seizure. She woke with a start, her face soaked in sweat, and pulled herself out of bed. She went to check on Charlie just to make sure he was still breathing.

She cracked open his door and heard the sound of his deep, even breaths. But it wasn't enough. She crept toward his bed and touched his forehead. Still no fever.

Stevie climbed back into her bed and tried to sleep again. All through the night, the flashbacks came, tormenting her with vivid details of the moment she only wanted to forget.

Before dawn on Friday morning, she gave up on sleep and threw the covers off her body. She raked her fingers through her hair. *How is it possible to be this tired and not be able to sleep?*

Stevie took a long, hot shower and then dressed in her favorite jeans and a long-sleeved cotton t-shirt. After pulling her shoulder length mane into a sloppy ponytail, she went downstairs and into the kitchen to make coffee, certain she could drink an entire pot by herself.

She had stacks of gluten-free pancakes prepared by the time Sam and Charlie arrived in the kitchen. Sam headed straight for the coffee maker while Charlie settled into his usual seat at the tile-topped table.

"Somebody's feeling better today." Sam added a heaping teaspoon of sugar to his mug.

"I can see that." Stevie smiled. "Charlie, would you like some pancakes?"

Her son nodded. She stole a glance at Sam, who flashed a broad grin. He appreciated Charlie's developmental leaps as much as she did. She suspected that he shared her giddiness over their son's new ability to nod his head in reply to a question.

Sam leaned over to Stevie. "Sometimes I ask him questions that I already know the answer to just to see him do it."

"Me too." Stevie giggled.

After breakfast, Sam took charge of cleaning the kitchen, as he'd so often done when he lived there. Stevie followed Charlie back upstairs to help him get dressed.

"Take off your pajamas." She stood with her back to him as she surveyed the contents of his dresser drawer. She selected a pair of jeans with an elastic waistband and a light sweatshirt featuring a silly picture of one of his favorite cartoon characters.

Stevie gasped as a vision of Charlie's blue, oxygen deprived skin zipped through her mind once more. She hunched forward, clutching her stomach. The image faded almost as soon as it had arrived, but it left a mark.

I can't keep reliving that moment. I just can't. Her hands shook as she loosened her grip on Charlie's clothes. She took in a deep breath in an attempt to calm the panic that rose within her body.

She straightened her shoulders, frustrated by her inability to control her own mind. She didn't want to think of the seizure at all. Why did it keep coming back to haunt her?

She forced herself to smile and then twirled around to hold up her selections for Charlie's approval. Not realizing he had come to stand right behind her, she jumped. Still in his pajamas, he stared in her direction, not quite making eye contact.

"Charlie, are you okay?"

He did not nod or offer any indication that he'd heard her. Instead, he stepped closer and grasped her hand.

As soon as he touched her, a wave of comfort flowed throughout her body. Her muscles relaxed as overwhelming peace washed away the images that had haunted her without mercy. She exhaled a great breath, savoring the unexpected solace.

Stevie's jaw dropped. "Did you do that?"

Charlie let go of her hand and nodded.

She blinked. There was so much she didn't know about her son. For years, she'd wondered how he felt, what he was thinking, and what he understood about the emotions of those around him. Now she knew he was not only capable of incredible empathy but also able to provide relief for the pain he sensed in others. "You knew I was hurting...and you helped me."

Charlie nodded again. "Magic."

"Yes, yes it is. What a wonderful gift you have, Charlie." Stevie wrapped her arms around her son. "Thank you."

After she helped him get dressed, Stevie left him to play with his Lincoln Logs. She went back to the kitchen and found Sam cleaning up the breakfast dishes. She watched him work, wishing she could tell him about their son's unusual gifts.

She refilled her coffee cup and propped herself against the counter. "I think I'll keep him home from school today, just to be on the safe side." Even though she knew Charlie was fine, his appearance in the classroom so soon after catching the flu would surely raise some eyebrows.

"Yeah, good idea." Sam finished loading their plates into the dishwasher. "Do you need me to stay? It's no problem."

"We'll be fine." She waved away his offer. "Thanks though."

Sam dried his hands and picked up his coffee mug. "Are we still on for tonight?"

"Um..." Stevie tilted her head. She had enjoyed having him around the night before, but maybe she'd given him the wrong impression. "On for what?"

Sam chuckled and patted her hand. "It's Friday, Stevie. He stays with me on the weekends. Remember? I figured that since he's not sick anymore, we would continue our usual routine."

"Oh." Stevie drew her mug up to her lips, hoping to hide her burning cheeks. "Yes, of course. No problem."

"Cool. I'll pick him up this afternoon after work." Sam draped the dishtowel over the handle on the oven. "Well, I guess I'll head out then."

Stevie trailed behind him to the front door and stepped out on the porch to say goodbye. "Thanks again for staying. You were a big help."

"I didn't do anything." Sam rubbed his neck. "I still can't get over how fast he recovered. Our kid is amazing."

Stevie smiled. "Yeah, he is." She couldn't tell Sam just how amazing Charlie was, but at least they could agree they'd created a spectacular little human.

He wrapped his arms around her. "Thank you for letting me stay. It was good to be here and good to know that we can still be parents together no matter what else is going on." He gave her a quick kiss on the cheek and backed away. "I'll see you later."

Stevie watched him walk to his truck. Maybe they had finally figured out how to manage life after the divorce. As he pulled away from the curb, she spun on her heels to go back inside. An unexpected sight forced her to stop mid-turn.

Dylan stood on his porch next door, glaring at her with such ferocity that Stevie's breath caught in her throat. She gulped as she realized what he must have been thinking when he saw Sam leave her house so early in the morning.

"You got my message!" Out of habit, she'd kept her mental shield up, even while he'd been away. She lowered it now so he could know there was nothing to worry about. "You wouldn't believe all that happened while you were away. Come on over. I'll tell you all about it." She gestured for him to join her.

Dylan ignored her words and her thoughts. He shook his head and stomped inside his house, slamming the door behind him.

Chapter twenty-nine

Stevie

Stevie tightened her grip on the steering wheel as she drove to Ruth's cottage on Saturday morning. A full day had passed since Dylan returned, and he still refused to see her. He hadn't even bothered to respond to any of her text and voice messages. She'd tried to be patient and give him time to come around, but now his behavior had gone from inexplicable to ridiculous.

He had to have heard her thoughts. Sam's too. *He must know that Sam was only there to help with Charlie.* She never would have expected Dylan to be so unreasonable.

She'd let him into her life—into Charlie's life—because she'd believed they had something special. Now she wondered if she really knew him at all.

She parked her Prius in Ruth's driveway, behind Randy's car, as thick clouds raced by overhead. The cool, overcast day matched her mood. She trudged up the walkway to Ruth's porch, listening to the dogs inside bark their warnings as she approached.

Ruth opened the door before Stevie had a chance to knock. "Come in."

Stevie followed the older witch into the house. She paused when she spotted Randy snoozing on the sofa. "Should I come back another time? I'd hate to wake him up."

Ruth, followed by her white pit bulls, continued on toward her kitchen. "Ah, don't worry about that. Alice prepared an extra-strong batch of her special sleeping tea. He's been taking a lot of naps since we heard about the amulet. He's trying to find it in a vision."

"Any luck?" Stevie quickened her steps to catch up to Ruth.

"He's having plenty of visions, but none of them have been useful." She shook her head. "He's very frustrated."

Stevie sighed. "That's too bad."

Ruth bent over and scratched one of her dogs on the head. "This is Gus." She leaned to her other side and stroked the back of the other dog. "This is Patsy."

Stevie bent down to scratch Patsy's head.

"No!" Ruth snatched Stevie's hand away. "Patsy likes to be stroked. Gus is the one who likes to have his head scratched."

"I'm sorry." Stevie snapped up and straightened her back. "I didn't realize that they were so particular."

Ruth glared at Stevie. "There's nothing wrong with knowing what you like." Patsy and Gus wagged their tails in agreement. "Now, let's get your training started."

"Do you really think I'll be able to talk to animals like you do?"

"Actually, I'm almost certain that you won't. I think you would have figured out that you had this ability by now. It was the first power I developed. Everything else came later." Ruth took a seat at her table. "Believe it or not, there was a time when all witches could do what I do. Our connection to nature gave us incredible power when it came to working with plants and animals. But now that our bloodlines have been diluted over the generations, communicating with animals has become a rare, special gift. It's just like Randy's visions and Alice's kitchen nonsense. Then there's whatever-the-hell it is that Deborah does with yarn..."

"She knits."

"I know that. I just think it's stupid." Ruth scowled.

Patsy and Gus sat at her feet, their tails wagging.

"When I communicate with animals, there's a back and forth. I can understand them, and they understand me. It's a telepathic connection. The best we can hope for you is that you will have the ability to compel an animal to do what you say. There's a difference. Now watch, I'm going to give each dog a different command without saying a word."

As Ruth narrowed her eyes, both dogs stopped wagging their tails, and their ears perked up.

In a blur of fur, Patsy bolted out of kitchen. Gus pranced over to the cabinet under the kitchen sink and nudged it open with his nose. He snapped up a small bag of dog treats and delivered them to Ruth. Patsy returned, carrying a pair of slippers in her mouth. She dropped them at her owner's feet. Ruth rewarded each one with a treat.

Before Stevie had a chance to react to the dogs' performance, Ruth went rigid. The old woman leaned toward Patsy, listening to something only she could hear. Then, she rushed out of the kitchen. "Something's wrong with Randy!"

Stevie followed her to the living room where they found Randy still asleep on the couch. Beads of sweat had formed on his forehead and above his lip. He rolled his head back and forth, as though he were witnessing something unfathomable. His chest heaved with rapid breaths.

"Randy!" Ruth gripped his shoulders and shook them. "Randy, wake up now!"

His eyes flew open, and he sat straight up. He took a frantic glance around the room and then settled his wide-eyed gaze on Ruth. "It's far worse than we thought."

Stevie's heart began to race. "Did you see the amulet?"

"Yes." Randy gave a hesitant nod. "On Susan."

Ruth slumped down on the sofa next to him. "No. This can't be happening."

Randy's frown deepened as he curled his arm around Ruth's thin shoulders.

Stevie tilted her head, perplexed by the couple's sadness. "Can't we just take it back? There are more of us, surely we can take her."

Ruth shook her head. "You don't get it."

Randy squinted at Stevie with red-rimmed eyes. "Honey, there's more power in that amulet than in all of us combined. There's no stopping Susan now."

Chapter thirty

Vanessa

Vanessa stood on the deck of her yacht, with her back to the town, listening to the sounds coming from Front Street. Shopping bags crinkled. Excited children squealed. Conversations, both boisterous and serene, echoed in the air. Life was happening right behind her. Without her.

She wanted to step off the yacht and visit one of the nearby shops, just to be part of the world—even if only for a few moments. But the horror of Susan's hallucination was still fresh in her mind. She shook her head, banishing the thought. She couldn't go anywhere. Not yet anyway.

She stared across the water to Carrot Island, where a herd of wild horses walked along the beach. Untamed and unfettered, they did as they pleased. Some stopped to graze on sea grass while others took to the water, splashing through the shallows without a care in the world. They had no obligations, no fears, only freedom. She watched one horse tilt his head in her direction as a breeze blew through. His mane fluttered up from his thick neck, dancing with the whims of the wind.

Vanessa reached up to touch her own hair, but her fingers sifted through empty air. She'd cut the remaining long tendrils from her head herself. What had once been a crown of long, lustrous black hair was now a mess of chopped and fuzzy patches scattered all over her scarred scalp. She tugged on her hood, making sure it was firmly in place.

Ice clinked against glass behind her. She turned to see her mother emerge from the cabin with a Bloody Mary in her hand. Susan sauntered to the opposite side of the deck and regarded the pedestrian traffic on Front Street with a smirk.

"Look at all those witches, just walking along like nothing has changed. They have no idea that they have a new queen." She raised her glass to her lips and took a long sip.

Vanessa kept her head low, peering at her mother from beneath the edge of her hood. "When do you plan to tell them?"

"After I have my fun with the coven." She twirled the celery stalk in her drink. "They'll all beg for my leadership then. It will make the transition much easier."

"I wouldn't underestimate the coven's power if I were you. Stevie, in particular, is very protective of her kid. She'll do anything to keep him safe."

Susan laughed and took another long sip of her drink. "All mothers are like that. I'd do the same for you."

Vanessa suppressed a snort and wondered how many drinks Susan had consumed before coming onto the deck. Her mother had never been anything like Stevie. Not even when Vanessa was a child. She couldn't recall a single time that her mother had protected her. Not then and certainly not now. If anything, Susan had thrown her to the wolves just to get what she wanted.

The way Vanessa saw it, Susan was just as responsible for her burns as Stevie was. Probably more so. But she kept these thoughts to herself. She didn't want to anger her mother again.

The overcast sky darkened as black storm clouds rolled in. A strong gust of wind blew through, and Vanessa held on to the edge of her hood to keep it in place.

"I do hope this weather clears up by tomorrow morning." Susan studied the clouds. "I have a very busy day planned."

Vanessa stared at her mother for a long moment, knowing there was nothing she could do or say to change her mind. The battle for Beaufort had already begun.

Chapter thirty-one

Stevie

Stevie paced the length of Ruth's living room. "How could Susan have gotten the amulet anyway? She's been in a psych ward for over a decade. Besides, Mom said it was a man who attacked her." She shook her head in disbelief. "This just doesn't make sense."

Ruth glanced at Randy. "Is there any chance that was just a dream?"

"It was so vivid." He rubbed the back of his neck. "It sure seemed like a real vision."

"I have an idea." Ruth stood up with a grunt. She crossed the room to a small desk, which sat beneath the window, and began rummaging through one of the drawers. "Let's call the loony bin. If she's still there, then we'll know it was just a dream." She produced a well-worn address book, opened it, and searched for the number she needed.

"Good thinking, Ruth." Randy's eyes lit up.

Ruth pressed the speaker button on her desktop telephone, and a dial tone buzzed for all to hear.

Stevie held her breath as the call rang through.

When a deeply southern female voice greeted her on the line, Ruth bent forward, closing the gap between herself and the phone. "I need to speak to Susan Moore. She's a patient there."

The hospital receptionist placed the call on hold, and sedate piano music tinkered through the speaker. Ruth drummed her fingernails on the desk while she waited.

The music stopped, leaving only silence on the line. Stevie heard a click and then a woman's voice spoke. "Who is this?"

Ruth cast a sidelong glance at Randy, who nodded in return. "It's her." She propped her hands on her hips. "You know who this is, Susan. I'm just calling to make sure you're still in there. Bye!"

"Wait!" The woman shouted before Ruth could disconnect the call. "I am not Susan! You have to get me out of here!"

Ruth snorted. "Well that's never going to happen."

"I am *not* Susan!" The voice screamed again. "I am…" A muffled skirmish ensued on the other end of the line. "Wait! Let me go!"

The receptionist's voice came on the line. "Ma'am? Are you still there?"

Ruth glanced at Stevie and Randy. "Yes. What's going on?"

In the background, falling farther and farther away, Susan continued shrieking. "I don't belong in here! I am not Susan!"

The woman cleared her throat. "Mrs. Moore has had a difficult day, as I'm sure you could tell. We have…uh…intervened. You might want to call back tomorrow."

Ruth disconnected and turned to Randy. "That was definitely her. I'd know the sound of her voice anywhere. You didn't have a vision. It was just a dream."

Randy exhaled and smiled. "I never thought I'd be happy to hear that voice again."

"Why was she saying those things?" Stevie tilted her head. "Isn't she magically compelled to only speak the truth?"

"Her idea of truth is only as accurate as her own perception." Randy shrugged. "She must really believe she's someone else."

Ruth swirled her finger in the air beside her temple. "Susan's always been a little…off."

"This is probably just a natural progression of her condition. She's right where she belongs." Randy sank back against the couch cushions and ran his hand through his hair. "At least now we know my vision was just a dream. I can't imagine anything worse than Susan having possession of the amulet."

Chapter thirty-two

Alice

Alice prepared for the Sunday morning service as she always did. She selected a modest dress with a floral print and slipped it on over her head. The dress fit tighter than it had the last time she wore it, but a few extra pounds were the least of her concerns now.

She'd always looked forward to the weekly church service. It was a time for worship and fellowship, two of her favorite things. No matter how heavy her heart was at eleven o'clock, she'd be smiling once more by noon. However, on this Sunday, her hands trembled as she touched the delicate gold cross on her neck.

Today, she would face the chaplain whom she'd so recklessly invited into their lives. If he was indeed the one who had stolen the amulet, what plans did he have for it?

She intended to invite him to her house for lunch, hoping to avoid a confrontation with the chaplain at church. She wouldn't tell him that Patricia would be there as well. Nor would she divulge that she planned to brew one of her special teas for him—one that would help him provide truthful answers to the many questions she and Patricia had. It was a far less obvious use of magic than working a truth spell on him. If he was innocent, then he would be none the wiser at the end of their talk. And if he was guilty...he'd have to answer to the queen. She swallowed hard. She had no idea how the coven would handle the matter of an outsider knowing their secret.

Alice mustered all of her courage and exited her house, double-checking the lock on the front door as she closed it behind her. Just as she began to make her way down the front steps, she spotted Stevie and Lexi waiting in her driveway.

In all of the excitement of the week, Alice had completely forgotten that she'd invited them to attend the service with her.

"Hello, girls." She waved as she approached them.

Stevie wore black dress pants and a simple cardigan set. Lexi wore a heavy, cowl-necked wool sweater that covered her from the bottom of her chin to the middle of her thighs. Her long denim skirt scraped across the concrete driveway as she stepped forward to greet Alice.

"I wasn't sure what attire would be appropriate." Lexi shrugged. "Is this okay?"

Stevie chuckled. "Apparently, Lexi thinks we're going to church in the nineteenth century."

Alice smiled and patted Lexi's shoulder. "It's just fine, dear. Jesus doesn't care what you wear, just that you show up." She glanced down at Lexi's heavy sweater. "I'm sure he appreciates the effort though."

They walked the short distance to the church on a sidewalk lined with southern live oaks and magnolia trees. The storm clouds from the day before had moved on, leaving them with a blue sky and a gentle breeze.

Alice wrung her hands as she ambled along with Stevie and Lexi, still fretting over the chaplain's intentions. She wondered if it had been a mistake to have them visit her church on a morning clouded with so much uncertainty.

She cleared her throat. "Girls, I don't know what to expect today. The pastor I had invited you to hear couldn't make it. Now, we have this chaplain who may have taken Patricia's amulet. If he's guilty…" She paused, searching for the best way to convey her concerns. "Please don't hold the actions of this one man against the entire church."

Stevie threw her arm around Alice's shoulders and offered a reassuring smile. "Of course not."

The three arrived at the old church and found Parris greeting parishioners at the front door. Alice studied him as he shook hands and welcomed everyone. She forced herself to continue toward him, weighed down by the guilt of her role in bringing him into their lives.

"Good morning, Chaplain." She gave a curt nod and a tight smile—the best she could offer under the circumstances.

His eyes narrowed just a bit before he offered a broad grin. "Alice, thank you for inviting me to preach this morning. I've been looking forward to this."

There was something different about him, but Alice couldn't quite put her finger on it. Uneasy under his piercing gaze, she shifted her weight from one foot to another. With effort, she managed to maintain her composure. She didn't want to give away any of her concerns. He had to believe that she didn't suspect him. Otherwise, he would almost certainly reject her lunch invitation when she offered it after the service.

She inhaled a deep breath, hoping he didn't notice the tension in her shoulders. "What is the focus of your sermon today?"

"I'd prefer to keep that a surprise." He winked. "But I guarantee it will be memorable."

A chill raced up Alice's spine. For the first time in her entire life, the thought of an upcoming sermon filled her with dread.

Chapter thirty-three

Patricia

Patricia sat in a rocking chair on her front porch gazing out over the green grass of her lawn. All traces of last night's thunderstorm had evaporated, except for a shrinking puddle on the sidewalk. She soaked in the warmth of the shining sun and breathed in the cool, salt-tinged breeze. The beauty of this calm Sunday morning was not lost on her, but it did little to ease the fears she had for her coven and all of the other gentle witches of Beaufort.

She hated herself for losing the amulet. Her ancestors had kept it safe for thousands of years, even through witch hunts and mass relocations. But she'd managed to lose it in a moment. One weak, helpless moment. She winced, remembering the sting of the stun gun.

All of her locator spells had failed, so she still didn't know where the amulet was or who had it. If a dark witch had taken it, its unparalleled power could yield total destruction. But in the hands of a non-witch, it was nothing more than a historical trinket. Regardless, the amulet belonged with her. She touched the bare space on her chest where the amethyst once resided. She had to get it back.

The front door creaked open, and Jim stepped out onto the porch carrying two cups of coffee. He passed one to Patricia and then settled into the rocking chair next to her.

They sat together in comfortable silence for a moment before she felt his gaze on her.

"What's going on?" His forehead wrinkled with concern. "You look a little pale. Are you feeling okay?"

Patricia patted his hand. "Oh, I'm fine."

She despised lying to him. There had been many times in their years together when she had teetered on the brink of telling him the truth. But she'd always held fast. She resisted the powerful urge even now, when she desperately wanted to share her heartache with him. "Fully recovered." At least that part was true.

He grunted a skeptical acknowledgment and took a sip of his steaming coffee. After decades of marriage, Patricia knew he wouldn't press for more information. She cupped her hands around her mug, seeking comfort in the warmth it provided. But there was no solace to be had. Not yet anyway.

Perhaps today she would be able to retrieve the amulet. Alice was in the process of setting their plan in motion. While she hoped Chaplain Parris accepted the invitation for lunch, she dreaded the thought of being in the same room with him. It would be worth the effort though. If everything went well, the amulet would be back in her possession by the end of the day. Then and only then would she be able to relax.

But if it didn't go well...

She tightened her grip on her mug, resisting the urge to go to the church and confront the chaplain right away. The drive to protect her people almost overwhelmed her. The compulsion had engulfed her the moment her mother died and the coven

170

members bowed to her as their new leader. Even now, in the absence of the magical amethyst, that innate drive remained just as strong. Her responsibilities as queen were a result of genetics, not jewelry. Nevertheless, without the amulet, her own magic was not bolstered enough to protect the others the way her instinct demanded.

She blinked back frustrated tears and thought of the queens who had come before her, those fierce hidden warriors who'd kept the amulet secure across the millennia. A lump grew in her throat. She'd failed them *and* her loyal coven. And if she didn't get the amethyst back, she'd fail Stevie, the future queen, as well.

Chapter thirty-four

Alice

Alice led Stevie and Lexi to her seat near the front of the church, waving to the familiar faces waiting among the pews as she passed by. With each step forward, she spotted more and more notable absences among the congregation. She cast a wary glance around the room. Only about half of the usual attendees were present.

"Here we are." Alice gestured for her guests to have a seat. Stevie and Lexi obeyed and filed into the pew. Alice slid in next to Lexi, taking the spot closest to the aisle.

She listened to the chatter echo throughout the sparsely filled sanctuary as families greeted one another. Members of the congregation exchanged handshakes and warm hugs while offering promises of prayers for sick relatives. She overheard several people blame the flu for the absence of many devout parishioners. In all her years, she'd never seen a flu outbreak affect so many people at once.

"The service will begin in just a few minutes." Alice glanced at Lexi. Noticing the tension in the young witch's shoulders, she patted her knee. "Relax, darling. Everyone in this room is guilty of something. Your sins are no worse than theirs."

Lexi shook her head. "It's not that." She kept her voice low and leaned in close to Alice. "I don't know why you and Patricia didn't pick up on it before, but that chaplain is a witch. I can see it in his aura. I'm certain of it."

A sudden coldness struck Alice, and she sunk back against the wooden pew. "Then the situation is far more serious than we thought." She clasped her hands together. "I have to put a stop to him now." She stood up, ready to confront Chaplain Parris who was still greeting parishioners at the door.

"We're coming too." Stevie rose from her seat as well. "You're going to need back up."

"Alice!" A familiar saccharine voice bellowed. "Hello!"

Alice pursed her lips. *Not now.* She twisted around to see Lynne barreling toward her. She glanced at her watch. There wasn't a minute to spare.

"Good to see you." Without success, Alice tried to catch a glimpse of the doorway where Parris stood. "But I'm sorry I can't chat right now. I need to speak to the chaplain." She stepped forward into the aisle, but Lynne blocked her.

"Oh, I see you've brought more guests with you!" Lynne peered around Alice to gawk at Stevie and Lexi. "I don't believe I've seen either one of you here before." Her tone was more of an accusation than a greeting.

Alice bristled under the woman's wolfish gaze. "We really have to get going now."

Lynne's smile broadened to reveal too many of her overly whitened teeth. "You should have a seat. The service is about to start. See?" She gestured toward the rear of the sanctuary. The chaplain had already entered and had begun to make his way down the aisle to the pulpit.

Alice cast a sidelong glance to Lexi and Stevie as Lynne moved away to take a seat behind them. "It's too late. We can't talk to him now without drawing attention." Dejected, Alice sunk into the pew. *There's nothing we can do now.*

She watched as men and women, spanning a variety of ages, filed into the choir loft behind the pulpit. Under normal circumstances the sight of this group, adorned in their simple blue robes, filled her with eager anticipation. She always enjoyed listening to the church choir. More than that, she loved singing along with them during the service. The fact that she couldn't carry a tune with any semblance of grace didn't stop her from putting her whole heart into belting out her favorite hymns. She cast a wistful glance at the hymnal stored on the back of the pew in front of her and sighed. She doubted today's service would be so satisfying.

With the exception of a mother's last minute reminder to her child to "hush," the sanctuary fell quiet. Alice locked her gaze on the chaplain, who pivoted around to the choir and nodded. The men and women in the loft stood and began the service with a familiar song of worship.

Alice narrowed her eyes. He hadn't carried a Bible in. What, she wondered, did he plan to preach about?

Lexi gently nudged Alice with her elbow. "Do you see his shoes?"

Alice swallowed hard as she took in the sight of his black tasseled loafers. Any remaining hope she'd held out for his innocence evaporated. Never, in her entire life, had she misjudged anyone the way she had him.

Upon completion of their song, the choir members sat back down. Instead of saying the customary opening prayer that she'd listed on the agenda for him, he stepped forward to speak to the congregation. *No Bible. No prayer.* Alice pursed her lips.

"I believe I met all of you out front before the service. But just in case I missed anyone, I am Chaplain Benjamin Parris." He smiled. "I'd like to thank Alice Gillikin for inviting me here today."

The hairs on the back of Alice's neck stood up as he fixed his gaze on her.

"On Sunday mornings, I usually deliver sermons to hospital patients. While I do miss my usual flock, I must confess that it's a treat for me to visit your church." He walked the length of the raised pulpit as he continued to talk. "I've spent the last several years of my life in Eastern North Carolina, but I have recently grown particularly fond of Beaufort. To some, this little town is nothing more than a mere dot on the state map. But we know, all of us here today, that it is *so* much more than that."

Stevie and Lexi exchanged a worried glance. The same anxiety churned within Alice. She crossed her legs and gripped her knee with both hands.

"Beaufort is a town steeped in rich and colorful history. Yet, it remains without pretense. Indeed, most would say what you see is what you get here in this community." The chaplain stopped walking and eyed the parishioners. "Am I right?"

Throughout the congregation, people nodded in silent agreement.

He raised his chin, holding his head high as though he were receiving the message of his sermon directly from heaven. He leveled his steely gaze on the congregation once more, and his amiable smile disappeared.

"Wrong!" He pounded his fist against the communion table.

"Oh dear." Alice gasped and clapped her hand over her mouth. The sanctuary filled with a flutter of surprised murmurs and confused whispers. She lowered her hand, but her body remained rigid. After several long moments, silence fell as the entire congregation sat in rapt attention. Everyone waited to hear what the chaplain would say next.

Chaplain Parris puffed out his chest. "I want you to think about the troubles you have in your life right now. Surely some of you are dealing with health problems." He arched an eyebrow and studied the faces of the parishioners. "Or maybe your family is struggling financially."

Across the aisle, Alice spotted several men and women leaning forward in their pews. She wrung her hands. The more Parris spoke, the more tangled the parishioners got in his net.

Maybe Lexi had been right. Maybe he did possess magic.

She glanced around again at the eager faces of her fellow churchgoers. They gazed upon the new chaplain as if he'd floated down from heaven on a fluffy white cloud, surrounded by angels with harps. But instead, he used the slick tongue of Satan to seduce them into whatever plot he had brewing.

Her stomach twisted. And she'd invited this fox into the hen house…

"Why do you think bad things happen to good people like you?" He extended his arms as though he were embracing everyone in the sanctuary.

Murmurs of uncertainty rose from the congregation.

"What if I told you that I knew why these terrible things were happening? What if I told you that I knew how to stop it all?"

Silence engulfed the room as everyone waited for him to go on.

Chaplain Parris stared down at the floor for a long moment before he raised his head. "What I'm going to tell you next will be hard to hear. Some of you might even think I'm crazy." He held his hand over his heart. "I assure you I am not."

He traced his finger along the edge of the communion table, dragging out the delicious agony of anticipation, and then took several slow steps across the front of the church.

Alice held her breath as he swaggered back to the center of the pulpit and licked his lips.

"Witches!" His threw his hands in the air and slammed them down on the table.

Alice jerked back as if he'd slapped her. *This can't be happening.*

More murmurs and gasps erupted from the congregation as the weight of the chaplain's proclamation reverberated throughout the church. Alice spotted a few parishioners shake their heads. Whether it was in denial or disbelief, she did not know.

Chaplain Parris gave a sincere nod as if to assure any doubters that his words were the gospel. "There are real, live witches right here in your pristine little town."

One hushed voice asked, "Is he serious?"

Another whispered, "There have always been stories, but I never thought they were real."

A withered old woman on the other side of the sanctuary turned to her husband. "Do you think the witches caused my angina?"

A lone voice rose up above the others. "I knew it!" Lynne's hot breath brushed against the back of Alice's neck.

Alice swallowed hard. Never before had she wanted to leave in the middle of a sermon, if that's what this abomination could be called. Her lower lip trembled. This place had always been her church, her sanctuary, her home. She loved these people as much as she loved her coven. They'd lifted each other up in times of sorrow. Celebrated together in times of joy. They were her family. Now, that comfort was lost, forever tainted by a man who would so easily turn on his own kind.

At least he hadn't called anyone specific out as witch. The festering fear and anger within the congregation wasn't directed at her. Not yet anyway. She leaned in close to Lexi and Stevie. "Sit tight, girls. Don't draw any attention to yourselves."

The younger witches nodded in silent acknowledgement, but the fear in their eyes spoke volumes. She had no doubt they already understood what she knew to be true; they were all witnessing the birth of a modern day witch hunt.

The chaplain offered a wry smile. "At the hospital in which I work, I met a patient who had suffered dearly under the wrath of a secret coven operating here in Beaufort. In fact, it was this group of sinister witches who had willfully disabled her. Leaving her to rot in that hospital for twelve long, unbearable years."

There was only one person who fit that bill. Alice pursed her lips. Until now, it had never occurred to her that he worked at a *psychiatric* hospital. Now she understood why he'd gone to Patricia's house in the first place.

"Think about that for a minute." Chaplain Parris pointed to the congregation. "If the witches are powerful and wicked enough to cause that sort of harm, don't you think it's possible that they could be behind this terrible flu outbreak?"

Alice ground her teeth. She fought the urge to defend herself and her coven with every bit of self-control she possessed. She curled her hands into a tight fist.

"I'm told that this unusually strong flu virus has impacted at least half of your congregation already." Chaplain Parris leaned against the communion table and crossed his arms. "Your own pastor has been afflicted with it! Are you going to allow these witches to harm your community in this way? Are you merely going to sit back while they flaunt their evil ways?"

"No! I most certainly will not!" Lynne shouted once again. A few loud calls of agreement came from parishioners scattered throughout the sanctuary.

The chaplain raised his fist in triumphant solidarity with Lynne before he scanned the full congregation once more. "The Bible gives us very clear direction regarding how to deal with a problem of this nature."

Chaplain Parris focused a taunting gaze on Alice. She squared her shoulders and glared back at him.

"Exodus 22:18." The chaplain recited the verse from memory. "Thou shalt not suffer a witch to live."

Alice turned away from pulpit and the crazy zealot behind it. She glanced around to the faces of her church family, assessing their reactions. Most of them remained stoic, as if they were watching any other sermon. She found it impossible to decipher if they'd been taken in by the chaplain's fervor or if they were simply indifferent to the thought of killing suspected witches. She wasn't sure which was worse.

But some perched on the edge of their seats, awaiting the next words from the chaplain.

How can they fall for this so easily?

"So you see, *you* have a responsibility to handle this infestation of witches in your town. He rubbed his hands together. "Otherwise, you'll burn in hell right along with them."

Alice hung her head as tears streamed down her face. She wished she could run away—as far away from the chaplain as she could get because she couldn't stand to listen to him slosh more fuel on the hate-filled fire he'd just ignited in the small church.

The sanctuary that had once been so full of faith, charity, and hope was now flooded with fear of brimstone and magic. And it had all happened in a matter of minutes.

Chapter thirty-five

Stevie

Patricia, Deborah, Alice, and Lexi sat around the table in Stevie's kitchen. A fresh pot of coffee finished brewing while Alice relayed the events of the morning's church service. Stevie filled four mugs and distributed one to each of her guests before pouring a cup for herself and joining them at the table.

Alice released a heavy sigh. "It was just awful, Patricia. I never imagined that we might have to face this sort of madness in this day and age. Certainly not from my own church." She blinked a fresh batch of tears that threatened to fall. "Needless to say, I didn't invite that man to my house for lunch. I simply couldn't." She shook her head. "I just wanted to get the girls out of there as fast as possible once the service ended."

Patricia patted Alice's hand. "I understand. That was the right thing to do."

"It was surreal. I can't believe how *fast* they turned on us. One minute, the choir was singing. The next, the chaplain was calling for death to all witches." Lexi gripped her coffee mug with both hands. "And those people just ate it up."

Alice traced the rim of her mug with her finger. "Not all of them. I'm sure there were some who…" Her voice cracked with unbearable sadness, and she did not bother to finish her sentence.

Stevie looked to her mother. "Is it possible that people have known about us all along? That chaplain didn't have to do much convincing. If anyone in that church had doubts about what he said, they sure kept quiet about it."

Patricia took in a deep breath. "This is how it begins. The reasonable stay silent while the hatred gets louder. Unfettered, paranoia takes root." She fixed her gaze on the window above the sink. "Did he say anything to implicate us specifically?"

Stevie shook her head. "No. As far as I could tell, the parishioners don't suspect us. But we know that the chaplain certainly does. If he decides to start naming names…" She couldn't bring herself to say it out loud. Charlie, her mother, Dylan, and the entire coven were at risk of discovery. Everyone she loved could be swept away in a lethal frenzy of ignorant paranoia. Her arm quaked as she raised her mug from the table, sending hot coffee splashing over the rim. She set it back down without taking a sip.

"I'll never forget the way he looked at me." Alice shuddered. "I still don't understand why he would do this. It was awful enough to steal the amulet, but why turn the town against us?"

"What could he possibly have to gain by risking the lives of his own people?" Deborah removed her knitting needles from her canvas bag and then rooted through the tote until she produced a skein of white yarn.

"It seems we have more questions than answers right now." Patricia spoke with the poise Stevie had come to associate with her mother, the queen.

While everyone else at the table succumbed to the effects of overwhelming fear, Patricia maintained a steady and calm appearance. Stevie knew she had to be frightened, or at least worried, but her mother showed no sign of it.

She'd been attacked in her own home, suffered the loss of the amulet, and now faced the unthinkable. Yet she sat with her shoulders squared and her chin high, giving the distraught coven members exactly what they needed—a leader in a time of crisis, regal in the face of what had to be her worst fear. The mere sight of her slowed Stevie's frantic breaths. She straightened her back, attempting to mirror her mother's example.

Deborah's knitting needles clicked as the conversation continued. Her hands moved with swift precision as she worked a new row of white yarn into her blanket. Stevie recognized this as a protection spell, but Deborah's furrowed brow gave away her own doubts of its efficacy.

"Randy is continuing to seek information through his visions, but he's been unsuccessful so far. My attempts to locate the amulet with magic have failed. Now that we know the chaplain is a witch, it's a safe bet that he's wearing it." Patricia glanced at Stevie. "It's a shame that Dylan is away. A good mind reader would be very helpful right now. Have you heard anything from him?"

"Oh, yes!" Alice's eyes lit up with hope. "When is he due to come back, dear?"

Caught off-guard, Stevie cleared her throat and shifted in her seat. "Actually, he *is* back. At least I think he's still in town. He may have gone back to London though. I haven't seen him since early Friday morning." She stared down at her coffee mug, avoiding Lexi's quizzical gaze. "He's upset with me. He's not answering my calls or my texts."

"I'll run next door and see if he's home now." Lexi pushed back her chair and stood up. "Once I explain what's going on, I'm sure he'll want to help."

"Good idea." Patricia nodded. "Please let him know that we're having a full coven meeting tomorrow night." She paused. "His attendance is mandatory."

"Will do." Lexi left the room.

Patricia fixed her gaze on Stevie and pointed at her. "I don't know what's going on with you two, but you're going to have to find a way to put it aside. You have to be able to work together. There are trying times ahead."

Stevie gulped. "I'm sure it won't be a problem." She knew she could put their issues aside to help keep their people safe. But, she couldn't really be sure how he would behave. Not after his overreaction to seeing Sam leave on Friday morning.

"Good." Patricia patted her hand against the tabletop. "We will need his help with the evacuation of Beaufort."

"What?" Stevie lurched forward, eyes wide. "We can't leave! This is our home!"

A long moment passed before Patricia replied. She faced her daughter with unwavering resolution. "With or without the amulet, my first priority is to protect all of you. Not only the members of our coven but all of the witches in this town."

Deborah lowered her knitting needles. "That's hundreds of people, Patricia. It's a sizeable chunk of Beaufort's population. How can we move that many families without someone taking notice?"

"I need time to sort out the details, but I'm certain it can be done." She shifted her gaze back to the window and sighed. "The world is different now. It's smaller and more connected. This will be a complicated endeavor to say the least. We'll discuss it further tomorrow night when we're all together."

In the ensuing silence, Stevie considered the magnitude of Patricia's words. Sacrifices for the greater good had long been a recurring theme in the history of their people, but the concept of a mass relocation was almost too much to imagine. Where would they go? How would they get away?

Stevie glimpsed the deep-set frown on Patricia's face, a crack in her calm façade. She reached across the table to squeeze her mother's hand.

Patricia tilted her head and gave Stevie a wry grin. "I know this must seem very strange to you now. Believe me, when you become queen, it will all make perfect sense."

Stevie sank back into her chair, uncomfortable with the idea of becoming queen herself. She couldn't imagine being able to take charge in a situation like this. Not only would she be unable to duplicate her mother's stoicism, she was certain she'd choose a different course of action. In spite of Patricia's experience and the centuries of history to support her plan, Stevie still didn't believe it was necessary to evacuate Beaufort.

"I understand your need to protect all of us. I really do. But there's absolutely no way our town government would ever sanction witch hunts and trials." Stevie crossed her arms. "We're talking about a handful of people who were easily swayed by the ranting of crazy chaplain. There's nothing they can do to us. This isn't 1692."

"1691." Patricia cleared her throat. "Our people were long gone from Salem Village by 1692."

Patricia placed her hand high on her chest, where the amulet once rested. "When I first wore the amethyst, I became fully aware of our history. I could see and feel the events of the past that tested us, challenged us, and changed us over time. The amulet's memories became my own memories, each as real to me as if I'd lived those moments myself. I know firsthand the agonies of the queens who came before me."

She sipped her coffee. "This knowledge serves as a tether. When a new queen rises, following the death of her predecessor, she's filled with a tremendous maternal love for her people. It's both beautiful and utterly overwhelming in its strength. It's also terrifying. A love that intense can easily devolve into rage and vengeance against any possible enemy if left unchecked. I believe the knowledge provided by the amulet gives the queen a necessary balance. It keeps us from acting on our emotions. We are meant to learn from our history so that we don't suffer the same consequences of past mistakes."

Patricia glanced at Stevie. "It was the amulet that made it possible for me to share the story of Queen Lucia so vividly with you." She nodded toward Alice and Deborah. "I'm sure you all remember the experience from when you joined the coven."

The witches remained silent as they nodded their affirmation.

"I have a similarly clear memory of the events in Salem. What you all learned in school was only part of the story. Without the amulet, I won't be able to show it to you. But I can certainly tell you about it."

Patricia took in a deep breath. "It was December of 1691, and a brutal winter had already fallen on Salem Village…" Her face drew tight under the torment of the memory as she relayed the story of Lucia's mother, Diana, and the townspeople who'd come for her.

"For her, as queen and protector, there was really only one option. While the mob raged outside her door, Diana slipped the amulet over her head and placed it on young Lucia. She told her daughter to gather the others and escape that night for she knew it was only a matter of time before they too would become targets."

"Such a terrible choice to make." Alice pinched up her face and shook her head.

Deep creases formed across Patricia's forehead. "She was hanged that night without a trial."

"You've never told this story before." Deborah had halted her knitting while she listened.

"Because it was too painful for me. I can feel Diana's torment, and I know Lucia's heartbreak. It's as if I lived through that terrible night myself."

Stevie had a few vague memories of studying the Salem Witch Trials in school. Though most of the details had long since faded from her mind, she knew more than just one witch had been accused and hanged during those dark days. "There were twenty people executed during the trials. If Lucia led the witches out of Salem, who were all of those people?"

"All innocents." Patricia gave a sweeping wave of her hand. "Diana was the only real witch they caught. I believe her hanging sparked the madness that resulted in the trials that came the following year."

"I've never seen Diana mentioned in any historical account of Salem." Deborah resumed her knitting, expanding the white section to include a second row.

"Of course not." Patricia's hand curled into a fist, but she held her voice steady. "What those people did that night was criminal. No one involved would have volunteered a written account of the event. By the next morning, Lucia and the others had evacuated the village. There was no one left with an interest to pursue charges against the perpetrators."

"And the reasonable people stayed silent." Alice winced and swallowed hard.

Patricia nodded. "Exactly."

Chapter thirty-six

Stevie

S tevie stood on her front porch and waved goodbye to Patricia, Alice, and Deborah. A knot twisted in her stomach as snippets of their emotional discussion raced through her mind. With Dylan angry at her and the coven's impending evacuation in the works, it took everything she had to maintain her composure. She wished she had even a smidge of her mother's grace. While Patricia managed to keep a cool head in the midst of turmoil, Stevie wanted to crawl into bed and sob.

The sight of Lexi strolling back from Dylan's house did nothing to bolster her mood. Her feelings for him had become more complex than ever. One minute, she craved his company, wanting nothing more than to clear the air between them and set everything back to where it once was. The next, she found herself wishing that he had gone back to London because the thought of him staying next door while refusing to see her was almost more than she could bear.

"You were gone long enough. Was he home?" Stevie propped a hand on her hip while Lexi climbed up the porch stairs.

Lexi shook her head. "No. I really don't think he has left for London, so I let myself in and took a look around." She wiggled her fingers to show that she had used magic to gain access to his house. "There are still clothes in the closet, food in the fridge, and the furniture hasn't been covered up. If he's gone, he's not planning on staying gone for long. I left him a note about the coven meeting."

Stevie grunted an acknowledgement and spun around to go back inside her house. Lexi followed her to the kitchen.

"That's a good thing, right?" Lexi extended her hands, palms up. "I mean, if he's still here…well, that means he hasn't left."

"Very insightful." Stevie collected some of the empty coffee mugs from the kitchen table to keep her hands, and mind, busy.

"So, are you going to tell me what's going on?" Lexi carried the remaining mugs from the table to the sink. "You didn't mention there was a problem."

Stevie opened the door to her dishwasher and began loading it. "He misunderstood something he saw, and now he's refusing to give me the opportunity to explain."

Lexi leaned against the counter and crossed her arms. "Details, please."

Stevie groaned and explained that Dylan had seen Sam leaving her house early in the morning after he had stayed over to help with Charlie. "I know what it looked like. I really do. But he could at least give me a chance to explain."

Lexi stood up straight and let her arms fall to her sides. "Hey, Dylan is a level-headed guy. I'm sure he'll come around."

"That's just it. I'm not sure I want him to anymore." Stevie finished loading the dishwasher and slammed it closed.

"Wait." Lexi's forehead creased. "You're mad at him?"

"Damn right I am!" Stevie's cheeks flushed hot with anger. "I don't even know how a mind reader could jump to the wrong conclusion, but he did. On top of that, he hasn't answered any of my calls or replied to my texts. His behavior is just childish. We could settle all of this with a quick conversation. But he's made that impossible. Honestly, I just feel stupid right now. I thought I loved him—now I think I never really knew him."

"You've known Dylan your whole life!"

"Not really. He was gone for many years." Stevie busied herself wiping down the already spotless countertop. "He left right after his mother was killed. That could have changed him. I know it would have changed me. When you think about it, I've really only known Dylan, *this Dylan*, for a few short weeks."

She draped the dishcloth on the side of the sink and stared through the window for a moment. "It's over between us."

Lexi let out a dramatic sigh, walked to the refrigerator, and opened the door. "You're out of wine."

"It's been a rough week."

Lexi closed the refrigerator door and twirled back around. "How much time do we have before Charlie gets back?"

Stevie glanced at her watch. "A few hours. Why?"

"Let's go to Backstreet." Lexi's mischievous grin dominated her oval face. "It'll be good for both of us."

Stevie couldn't think of a single reason not to go.

Chapter thirty-seven

Stevie

Stevie scanned the dimly lit, uncrowded pub. A few determined drinkers were scattered around the bar, while a middle-aged couple lounged at a corner table watching the football game. She and Lexi claimed two stools near the center of the bar and ordered chardonnays.

A young blond woman descended the spiral staircase and placed an order for a microbrew. She smiled at them before going back upstairs.

"She's one of us," Lexi whispered.

Stevie nodded in silent acknowledgement. She didn't think she would ever get used to the concept of so many witches living among the locals. And yet, here she was, sitting in a bar frequented by both normal and magically gifted residents.

Even before her initiation into the coven, Stevie had known this town was special—she just hadn't known *how* special it was. She didn't want to leave. With a wistful sigh, she accepted the plastic cup of chilled wine from the bartender.

"Drink up." Lexi raised her cup in a toast to nothing in particular.

Needing no further encouragement, Stevie took a long sip of her chardonnay and rested the cup on the old, wooden bar. "It's awful quiet in here today."

"Uh-huh." Lexi scanned the room and her brow furrowed. "Drink faster."

"What's the rush?" Stevie glanced at her watch. "We have plenty of time."

"Trust me." Lexi's face had gone pale, and her hand trembled as she clutched her drink.

Stevie gripped her arm. "What's wrong? Are you okay?"

Lexi did not respond. She gulped her wine and plopped the empty cup to the bar. "Let's get out of here."

Stevie took another look around the sparsely populated bar, wondering what Lexi had seen that was so distressing. The few men sitting at the bar were all glaring at her. Even the couple who'd been watching football from the corner table bore through her with steely gazes. She stifled a gasp. There wasn't a friendly smile or a kind face in the entire room.

She and Lexi were lambs surrounded by a pack of wolves.

Keeping her head down as though it somehow protected her from the scrutiny of all of those hostile eyes on her, Stevie pulled some cash from her pocket and left it for the bartender. Without a word, she grabbed Lexi's hand, and they marched out of the pub without glancing back.

Her mother had been right. The hysteria had already begun to spread, and it was catching faster than the flu.

Once outside, they both squinted from the bright sunlight. Though her eyes had not yet had time to adjust, Stevie didn't stop. She hastened her steps as much as possible, resisting the urge to break into an attention-grabbing sprint toward her home. Lexi walked alongside her, keeping up with her brisk pace. Once they made it to Front Street, Stevie dared to look behind them. She didn't see anyone from the pub, but that did nothing to calm her nerves. She kept going.

"Were all of those people at the church this morning?" Lexi sputtered, trying to catch her breath.

"I don't think so, but I couldn't say for sure." Stevie continued her rapid pace. She wanted to put as much distance between them and the pub as possible.

"Then how did they know about us?"

"Chaplain Parris must have identified us to someone." Stevie's breaths came in shallow, jagged gasps. "It's a small town, word travels fast."

Stevie looked over her shoulder once again. No one had followed them. Wanting to blend in with the pedestrian traffic as much as possible, she slowed to a more casual pace.

The trip home only took a few minutes, and they passed several familiar faces along the way. Stevie spotted the librarian walking her little dog on the opposite side of the road. She had always been sweet to Charlie when they visited the library, often taking the time to make thoughtful book suggestions for him. Stevie's spirits rose when the woman smiled and waved. She waved back, relieved that she had not been taken in by the talk of witch hunts.

Not yet anyway.

The hostility at Backstreet had left Stevie with an overwhelming desire to connect with people who didn't hate her, so she continued to scan the sidewalk for familiar faces. In front of the Maritime Museum, she spotted her pharmacist. He'd always been kind to her. Buoyed by the cheerful greeting of the librarian, she waved to him as they drew near. "Hi, Mr. Johnson."

The old man cast a wary glance in Stevie's direction and then looked down without acknowledging her. He studied the sidewalk as though it was the most fascinating thing he had ever encountered.

As soon as they passed him, Lexi let out a low whimper. "I can't believe this is happening. These are good people. Why are they buying into the hysteria so easily?"

"It happened even faster in Salem. I suppose we should consider ourselves lucky." Stevie swallowed hard. "We'll have to tell my mom about Backstreet. She needs to know."

Stevie's house came into view as they continued down Front Street. Spotting someone on her porch, she pursed her lips. "Dylan's waiting for us."

"Good. Now you two can sort out your misunderstanding."

"He probably saw your note." Stevie shrugged as she made her way toward her house. "I'm sure he's not waiting for me."

Seeing Dylan was the last thing she needed. She was angry, and she knew he would be too. In light of everything that was going on in her beloved hometown, her romantic life was at the bottom of her list of priorities. If he hadn't been so unreasonable, she might feel differently. But there was nothing she could do about that now.

"Try to be nice," Lexi whispered as she opened the front gate.

They both stopped in their tracks as they caught sight of the entrance to Stevie's house. Someone had scrawled the word "witch" in bold red paint on the black door. Hot tears welled up in Stevie's eyes. Someone, perhaps even someone she knew, held so much hatred toward her that he or she felt compelled to vandalize her home. The cosmetic damage was insignificant compared to the act itself. Her gaze drifted to Dylan, who stood on her porch with his arms crossed.

"Can somebody tell me what the hell is going on in this town? They hit my house too." He clenched his jaw clenched as he awaited a response.

They joined him on the porch, and Lexi began to explain the unthinkable events of the day. Stevie crossed to the far railing to get a look at Dylan's door. It too bore the word "witch" in red paint.

"We need to clean this off before Charlie gets home." Stevie gestured toward the door. "I don't want him to see it." She struggled to keep her face impassive and her voice steady as she spoke, hiding the panic that bubbled within her.

"That's easy enough." Lexi stepped in front of the door and faced it straight on.

Stevie watched as her friend's brow knotted in intense con-centration. Lexi raised her right hand in front of her body. She positioned herself as though she were holding a large paint-brush. In one graceful movement, she swiped the invisible brush across the door. Fresh black paint covered the top half of the red word. She took another swipe, and the bottom half of the word disappeared. "There." She stepped back to assess her work. "It's all gone now."

No trace of the vandalism remained, except for Stevie's heartbreak. "Thanks, Lexi."

"No problem." Lexi turned to Dylan. "You want me to fix yours too? It's no trouble."

"Yeah." Dylan's response resembled a grunt more than a re-ply. "Thanks."

Without as much as a glance in Stevie's direction, he trailed behind Lexi as she descended the steps.

Stevie considered lowering her mental shield so Dylan could hear her thoughts. He would be unable to stop the flow of in-formation while they were in close proximity. Then he would understand he had no reason to be angry with her. He would know the truth. She watched him walk away. Each step he took represented another mile between them.

Stevie crossed her arms. No. He'd been a jerk. He didn't deserve to hear her thoughts. She propped her hands on her hips and tried to deny the gnawing ache in her heart. *What had happened to him? To us?* She couldn't go on like this. She had to talk to him.

"Dylan," Stevie called as he reached the gate at the end of her walkway. "Wait."

He stopped walking and spun around, his gaze dispassionate. "What?"

Staring into his cold eyes, Stevie's heartbreak gave way to a renewed anger. She thought of all that had happened that week, from Charlie's seizure to the fiasco at church just that morning. With each crisis, she'd only wanted to feel his arms around her. She'd wanted to bury her face in his chest and block out the world. But she couldn't tell him those things now. He'd chosen to be angry about an entirely wrong assumption. He'd chosen to end what they had in this most ridiculous fashion. Dylan had shut her out, without even giving her a chance to explain.

He wasn't the person she'd thought he was. He wasn't the man she'd loved.

"Never mind."

Chapter thirty-eight

Stevie

Stevie heaved a relieved sigh when Sam returned with Charlie on Sunday afternoon. Glad to have her son back in her care after the unsettling events of the day, she knelt down to his eye level and flashed the brightest smile she could muster. She ruffled his blond curls and planted a kiss on his forehead. "I love you."

Offering no response to this warm greeting, Charlie walked up the stairs to his room carrying his tablet.

Stevie stood alone with Sam in the foyer, unable to look at him. She didn't want to take Charlie from him. But with the coven's evacuation plan, she didn't have a choice. At the rate things were going, they'd have to leave Beaufort soon. And she couldn't say anything to him about it.

Charlie needed his dad, and Sam had a right to be with Charlie. They'd only just figured out how to manage co-parenting, and now she'd have to throw it all away. She bit her lip, wishing she could invite him to leave town with them. But that would raise questions she couldn't answer, and he might try to stop her from leaving with their son. She couldn't risk legal fall-out any more than she could expose her magical heritage.

"Stevie, are you okay?" He placed a hand on her shoulder and gazed into her eyes.

"Oh, yeah. I'm fine." She offered a thin smile. "Just a little tired."

Sam removed his hand but continued to study her face. "Uh-huh." He narrowed his gaze, dubious. "Anything you want to talk about?"

"No. It's nothing." She waved away his concerns.

"Okay. I guess I'll get going then." He reached for the door-knob. "You know I'm here for you if you need anything, right?"

Stevie smiled, a genuine one this time. "Of course I know."

Sam stepped out onto the porch, looked up at the bold colors of the sky, and whistled. "Maybe you should get a picture of that sunset, Stevie. It's one of the prettiest I've ever seen."

"I can do better than that." Stevie took in the strokes of orange and red painted by the setting sun. "I think I'll sit out here and watch it for a bit." She stepped over to one of the rocking chairs and positioned it so it faced west. "Care to join me?"

"Yeah, sure." Sam pulled a rocker next to Stevie's and sat down beside her.

Stevie cast a sidelong glance at Dylan's house, wondering if he knew that Sam was with her now.

What he thinks doesn't matter. At all.

"You sure you're okay?" Sam followed her gaze.

"It's just been one long, strange day." Stevie looked to the sky once more. "I went to church with Alice this morning." She paused, considering the safest way to describe what had happened without implicating herself or the others. "It got weird really fast. They had a guest speaker, a chaplain, who claimed that there are witches in Beaufort."

Sam chuckled. "Witches? Give me a break!"

"Well, he seemed to be looking to stir up some trouble here. He went so far as to suggest that witches should be killed."

"What a nut job." Sam's smile faded. "I'm sure the whole congregation thought he was crazy."

"That's just it." Stevie rubbed the tense knot in her neck. "Some of those people seemed to really like the idea. Have you heard any talk about it today?"

"Not a word." Sam shook his head. "I'm sure it'll die down, if it hasn't already. We might have a few people around here with questionable mental health, but it's not like the whole town is going to buy into that nonsense. Who are they going to go after anyway? Everybody knows witches aren't real!"

Stevie drew in a deep breath and looked back at the colorful sky. Maybe the witch hunt madness wasn't as widespread as she thought. Maybe they had more time.

Chapter thirty-nine

Stevie

That evening, Stevie tucked Charlie into his bed. He lay flat on his back, eyes wide open, staring at the ceiling. It was how he started out every night. She knew, as soon as the lights went out and the house was quiet, he would close his eyes and drift off. Once asleep he'd ease into a more comfortable position, which usually meant rolling over onto his side with the top edge of his blue comforter bunched up in his arms.

Stevie sighed, remembering those tough years when he'd had so much trouble at night. Every single night had been a challenge. He either took forever to fall asleep, or he couldn't stay asleep for long. Most nights, it was both. Of all of the difficulties that came with his autism diagnosis, that had been one of the most trying.

She and Sam had struggled under the effects of ongoing exhaustion as those sleepless nights evolved into sleepless months. Stevie blinked, recalling the cloying hopelessness she'd endured during those difficult days. That was when the cracks in the foundation of their marriage had begun to show. There'd been so much fighting. So many tears.

But things were better now for Charlie. She was filled to bursting with gratitude for all of his progress. But what if it had happened sooner? What if she and Sam had held on just a little longer?

She shook off the thought and brushed a stray curl from Charlie's forehead before giving him a kiss. "I love you. More than anything in the whole world." She crossed his room and flicked off the light switch. "Good night."

Stevie closed the door behind her and propped herself against it. In that moment, she became aware of the unmitigated exhaustion that had crept into her body. All she wanted to do was climb into bed and let all her worries fall away for a few hours, but she still had to turn off the lights downstairs and check the locks. With a yawn, she peeled herself away from Charlie's door and plodded toward the landing.

She stopped before her foot hit the first step as an unexpected idea occurred to her. Stevie closed her eyes and envisioned the knob on the front door. She visualized the lock twisting on its own until she heard it click into place. She did the same thing for the back door. With another burst of concentration, all of the downstairs lights clicked off. When there was nothing but darkness at the foot of the stairs, she padded toward her own bedroom.

As soon as she settled into her cozy bed and pulled the warm covers up to her chin, her mind began to race. Witch hysteria, leaving Beaufort, abandoning her home and business, taking Charlie away from Sam. *Dylan.* It was all too much. Her mind refused to let her rest.

She tossed and turned for almost an hour before giving up on sleep. *Maybe a cup of tea will help.* Since she didn't have any of Alice's magic concoctions in the house, chamomile would have to do.

Stevie sat up in bed, weighing the pros and cons of attempting to produce a steaming mug of tea out of thin air. Considering the multitude of ways that it could go wrong, she decided to make it the old-fashioned way. Besides, she found the ritual of making hot tea almost as soothing as the drink itself. She slipped out of bed and pulled on her terry cloth bathrobe.

She tiptoed down the hall toward the landing. She didn't want to wake Charlie. One insomniac tonight was enough.

She'd made it a little more than halfway down the steps when a rustling sound at the door stopped her cold. Had the vandal come back?

Fueled by both anger and curiosity, she raced down the remaining steps. She unlocked the front door and threw it open, expecting to catch the vandal in the act of defacing her home again. Instead, a piece of paper fell to her feet. A dark hooded figure stood on her porch, shrouded in the dim light offered by the moon. Stevie couldn't tell if her uninvited guest was a man or a woman. The figure began to back away, inching toward the steps.

"Stay right there!" Stevie bent down to retrieve the paper that had slipped out of the door.

The figure froze in place.

Stevie arched her brow, surprised. She hadn't expected the visitor to do as she commanded. She listened to the rapid breaths coming from beneath the hood. *Fear.* Whoever it was must have known she was a witch.

Stevie unfolded the paper.

TAKE THE BOY AND LEAVE BEAUFORT.

"What is this?" Stevie stepped closer to the dark figure. "Is this some kind of a threat?"

The figure did not look up, responding only with a subtle shake of the head.

"Look at me, dammit!" Stevie reached out and grabbed the strange visitor's left arm.

"No!"

Stevie had heard that voice before—a woman, someone she knew. She squeezed tighter. "Who are you?"

A pained whimper emerged from the woman as she struggled to break free from Stevie's grip. "Please, let me go. You're hurting me." Agony tinged her ragged voice.

"Okay. But you better start talking." Stevie released her grip.

The woman gasped and clutched her arm close to her chest. She kept her head low, maintaining the cover of her hood. "That note is not a threat. Only a warning. You need to take the boy and go. Go far away from here."

The woman's raspy whisper disguised her voice, but it was familiar nonetheless. It reminded Stevie of…

No.

She couldn't bring herself to even think the woman's name. She banished the thought. *Impossible.*

Whoever stood before her now knew Charlie. Her concern for him had to be genuine. Why else would she risk delivering this note?

"Who are you?" Stevie softened her tone, even as she considered removing her mysterious visitor's hood herself.

The woman glanced east, toward the docks on Front Street. She straightened, facing forward again, but her features remained hidden in the shadows. "I'm not here to hurt you. I came only to warn you." She gripped both sides of her hood. "Remember that."

Stevie's stomach clenched as the woman eased the dark hood back, revealing a short, choppy haircut marked by scattered bald spots concentrated on the left side of her scalp. Stevie caught sight of even more scars, horrible scars, marring her face. When the visitor raised her head, Stevie looked into her eyes. Her emerald green eyes.

"Vanessa!" Stevie tightened her hands into fists as she prepared to battle the evil witch again. "You're supposed to be dead."

"Sorry to disappoint you." Vanessa gazed back at her, calm and brazen. "Believe me, the fact that I still draw breath is often a disappointment to me too."

Though Vanessa's candor surprised her, Stevie refused to let her guard down. She waved the paper in her face. "What is this about? What are you trying to do to us now?"

"I'm trying to help you keep Charlie safe."

Hearing her son's name on this woman's lips only fueled Stevie's rage. She lurched forward. "What do you care about him? You tried to kill him!"

Vanessa didn't flinch. "Before you took away all of my power, I was one of the strongest witches alive. Don't you think if I had wanted to kill him, I would have?"

Stevie considered this for a moment. "I have no way of knowing what your plan was then. You might not have hurt him physically, but you certainly terrorized him."

"And that was regrettable." Vanessa's voice drifted as she glanced away. "I know you have no reason to trust me now." She sucked in a deep breath. "But I know for a fact this witch hunt craze is about to get far more serious. Charlie will be caught in the middle of it. He could get hurt."

"How do you know this?" Stevie narrowed her eyes.

Vanessa pulled her hood back into position. "That's all I can say. Just get him out of here." She began to walk away but came to an abrupt stop. She turned back to Stevie, and their eyes met once more. "Please don't tell anyone I was here."

Too stunned to do anything, Stevie didn't stop Vanessa as she slipped into the shadows.

Chapter forty

Stevie

The next day, Stevie tidied her already clean house, trying to keep her hands busy and her mind quiet—to no avail. No matter how hard she worked, she couldn't stop Vanessa's visit from haunting her thoughts. For weeks, she'd carried the burden of believing she'd killed the dark witch, but seeing Vanessa alive had done nothing to assuage her guilt. If anything, the sight of the woman's scars only added to her remorse.

She fluffed a pillow and placed it on the sofa, recalling Vanessa's reaction when she had gripped her arm. She hadn't applied that much pressure, and yet it seemed to cause terrible pain. *Burns.* She probably had them on her arm too. Stevie winced at the thought of the suffering she must have caused by blowing up the boat that night. Did anyone deserve to suffer like that?

It was self-defense. Vanessa had shot Dylan and gone after Charlie. Who knows what else she would have done if given the opportunity? The entire coven had agreed her actions that night were justified.

But it would be a lot easier to convince herself of her own righteousness if Vanessa hadn't come to warn her.

She had not yet told anyone of her late night visitor. Aside from the obvious shocking news of Vanessa's return, there was the puzzling element of the nature of her visit. Why had she come here to warn Stevie? She must have known how dangerous that was. Why would she suddenly be concerned about Charlie's well-being?

She wasn't sure when or how it had happened, but everything that had once been true was no longer. Her picturesque, serene, safe haven of a town had begun to transform into her worst nightmare. Fear and anger had become her constant companions. She now lived in a world in which Dylan turned his back on her and Vanessa showed concern for Charlie.

Nothing made sense anymore.

A knock on the door pulled Stevie out of her swirling thoughts. She opened it to find her mother standing on the front porch.

"Hello, dear." Patricia offered a sad smile. "I know I'm early, but we need to talk. Is Charlie home?"

Stevie stepped out of the way to allow her mother room to pass. "He's upstairs playing with his Lincoln Logs." She noticed Patricia's puffy, red-rimmed eyes. "Has something else happened?"

"No." Patricia made her way into the living room. "I just want to go over some things with you before the meeting tonight. We have a lot to talk about." She settled on the sofa and patted the seat next to her. "Sit."

Stevie complied and waited in silence for her mother to speak.

Patricia drew in a deep breath and met Stevie's gaze. "I'm afraid that the late development of your powers has left us with limited time to handle your training. In the past, the education of would-be queens began in childhood. It offered far more time than you and I have had to work together. Your development as a witch has only just begun, and so much has happened already…" She glanced away.

"I wish I could share with you the full history of our people throughout the millennia. Then you would understand, truly understand, how dire the situation is that we face now. Perhaps one day, we'll have our amulet back so you can witness the events of days gone by, as I have." She fell silent.

With a heavy sigh, she took Stevie's hand in hers. "We've been called many things throughout the ages: witches, wizards, healers, mystics, and sorceresses. There was a time when those names were the highest compliment. In ancient days, kings and queens relied on our counsel. People revered us for our healing abilities, for our unique understanding of nature, and for our celestial knowledge. If a witch visited a family home, the master of that household relinquished his seat at the head of the table without hesitation. That honor was bestowed on the witch, even if she happened to be a woman. They respected our kind then. But times changed, Stevie. What was once welcomed and appreciated has become feared and hated."

Stevie shook her head. "If they only knew the truth about us—that we are committed to harm no one."

Patricia's frown was grim. "No, my dear. Once the hysteria takes hold, you can't reason with them. You can only hide."

Stevie's stomach churned. *This is really happening.*

"In every new home our people made, they enjoyed long periods of peace, just as we have here. Eventually, and often without warning, the massacres began again. This is our burden to bear. It's our secret to keep. And because we possess such great power, it's ultimately our peace to make. We will not fight them. We'll run from them." Patricia tilted her head forward. "Do you understand?"

As much as she wished she could, Stevie couldn't deny her mother's wisdom on this matter. She nodded in acknowledgement.

"Our peaceful nature was, at one time, innate. After centuries of intermingling with non-witches, it seems that natural instinct has faded out of our genes. Now, our nonviolent and self-sacrificing ways must be taught consistently if we are to remain who we are.

"Take, for example, your experience with Vanessa. You lived for thirty years without magical gifts and without the benefit of training. Your solution was to destroy her by blowing up that boat. While I don't blame you for that decision, I know it's not a choice that I would have made. When we dealt with the problem of Susan years earlier, we didn't kill her, even though she had done the unthinkable. Instead, we took away her powers and secured her in a psychiatric facility. We avoided violence."

Stevie cringed at the memory of that night, made all the more painful after seeing Vanessa's scars.

"Why are we discussing this now?" She tugged on the hem of her t-shirt. "There are so many other things we have to worry about."

Patricia smiled. "Because you must fully comprehend our history and our peaceful nature in order to be a successful queen."

"Mom, we have plenty of time to discuss these things. You have years to re-educate me."

A tear fell down Patricia's cheek. "No. Our time together is nearing an end."

"What are you talking about?"

"I've decided to divide our people, just like Lucia did when Blackbeard arrived on her island. You will lead our coven, along with the solitary practitioners who wish to leave, to their new home. This relocation will be voluntary for all except for our coven members. I'll make sure the other witches know what's at stake if they choose to stay behind. I'm going to stay here, with your father, so I can retrieve our amulet. I can't do that *and* lead the evacuation."

Stevie shook her head. "But I want to stay with you. I can help you get the amulet back."

Patricia placed her hand on Stevie's knee. "We have to protect our family line—the original queen's bloodline. With the talk of killing witches, it's just not safe for you to stay here. You and Charlie have to leave Beaufort tonight, after the meeting."

"Tonight? I'm not ready! I haven't packed. I haven't talked to Sam about this." Tears spilled unfettered as the words tumbled out of Stevie's mouth. "Mom, I'm not ready to be a leader."

Patricia extended her arms, and Stevie sank into her embrace. Her shoulders shook as she sobbed, but her mother held her tight.

After a few moments, Stevie pulled away and wiped the tears from her cheeks.

"Charlotte felt the same way, my dear." Patricia raised Stevie's chin, forcing her to meet her gaze. "And look what she accomplished." She gave a broad sweep of her hand, gesturing around the historic home that had once belonged to Beaufort's first witch queen. "Our people have enjoyed three hundred years of peace in this wonderful place. You will find that again. I'm positive that, one day, your legacy will be just as marvelous as Charlotte's."

Chapter forty-one

Stevie

Tears welled in Stevie's eyes as she crammed a handful of t-shirts into her suitcase. She couldn't do anything to prepare Sam for what was coming. With no viable plan for visitation and no reasonable explanation for her departure with Charlie, she couldn't tell him about the evacuation. *It's just as well.* She sighed. She wasn't strong enough to face him now anyway.

With Patricia staying behind, she knew Sam would go to her first in search of his son. What would she tell him? Stevie grimaced. *Lies piled upon secrets.*

Maybe she could call Sam in a day or two and tell him they'd gone on an impromptu vacation. That way he wouldn't worry so much. But then what? Another call a week later just to say that they'd extended their stay? She shook her head, banishing that foolish idea. They weren't coming back, and Sam would never be satisfied with phone calls. He'd want to see his son. He had a *right* to see his son.

But I have to protect Charlie. She zipped her suitcase closed and stood up straight. *This is the only way.*

She had not yet told Charlie that they were leaving. Since he didn't handle uncertainty well, it was best to say nothing until she knew where they were going. All of the unknowns didn't sit well with her either.

She tucked her suitcase in her closet and crossed the hall to Charlie's bedroom. He stood at the table on the far side of the room, continuing his work on his latest Lincoln Log village.

"It's time for dinner." She cast a wistful glance around his comfortable room. *Where will Charlie sleep tonight?*

He followed her down the stairs and into the kitchen. She reheated some leftovers and set the plate in front of him. Without a word, she mixed his nutritional supplements in some apple juice and left that for him as well. "I've got to run upstairs for a few minutes. I'll be right back."

Stevie raced back up the steps and returned to Charlie's bedroom to pack a small bag for him while he ate his dinner. She grabbed a few outfits and some pajamas. *What else?* Spotting his Lincoln Log creations, her shoulders slumped. They'd have to leave all that behind.

She stowed his bag in her closet along with her suitcase and then hustled back to the kitchen.

Charlie poked at what remained of his dinner. Deep creases ran along his forehead as he pushed a bite-sized piece of chicken around his plate. She had no doubt that he sensed her anxiety. But there was nothing she could do about it now.

She glanced at her watch. "The Historic Society is meeting here tonight. It's going to be a lot of boring, grown-up talk." She forced a nonchalant wave. "You can play in your room while we meet down here." It would be anything but boring, but she didn't want Charlie to overhear their plans.

And I don't want him to see Dylan either.

213

Dylan's behavior had been so...unpredictable. If he was as rude to Charlie as he had been to her, she might not be able to maintain the peaceful demeanor that her mother wanted her to have.

Stevie heard her front door creak open. She poked her head around the corner to see Patricia letting herself in. Her mother had gone for a walk on the waterfront to clear her head before the meeting. The strain of worry was still evident in her grim expression, nothing at all like the calm veneer she'd presented to the other coven members.

"You left your door unlocked. That's not safe." Patricia closed, and locked, the door behind her.

Stevie walked the length of the hallway to join her mother in the foyer. "I don't think a locked door is going to stop our amulet-stealing psycho chaplain."

"But it might stop a non-witch from gaining entry. There's no telling how big his following has grown in the last twenty-four hours." Patricia grabbed Stevie and gave her a fierce hug. "I just worry about you. I can't help it." She smiled as she pulled away. "Now, where's my grandson?"

Stevie pointed down the hall. "I haven't told him yet. Please be careful what you say."

"Of course." Patricia made her way to the kitchen with Stevie trailing behind her.

Having finished his dinner, Charlie pushed back his chair and stood up as they entered the room.

Patricia squatted down so she was at eye level with her grandson. "Can you look at me, Charlie? Just for a second?"

Standing behind Charlie, Stevie couldn't see his eyes. From the angle of his head and the smile on her mother's face, she suspected that he had, in fact, made eye contact.

"My good boy." Patricia wrapped her arms around Charlie's small frame. "I just want to hold you for a moment. Is that okay?"

Charlie nodded. His arms remained at his sides, but he rested his head on his grandmother's shoulder. Stevie pressed her hand against her thudding heart, fearing it might snap in two.

Patricia glanced up with a watery gaze before she closed her eyes and squeezed Charlie tighter.

Stevie bit her quivering lip in an effort to hold back the torrent of emotion that boiled within her. But the sight of Patricia's silent goodbye was too much to bear. Her tears defied her will and streamed down her face anyway. Without a word, she hustled out of the kitchen to clean herself up. She didn't want Charlie to see her cry.

When Stevie came back, Patricia released Charlie. "Go play now. This meeting is going to be a bunch of boring, grown-up talk."

Stevie turned to her mother as Charlie headed up the stairs to his room. "I said the exact same thing to him."

"That's probably because it's what I used to tell you when you were little." The corners of Patricia's mouth curled up in a sad grin. "Maybe you did learn a few things from me after all."

Stevie bit her lip. *I hope so.*

When the doorbell rang, Stevie walked to the foyer to let Deborah, Lexi, Ruth, Randy, and Alice in. Without wasting a moment, they all found seats in the living room and waited in somber silence for the meeting to begin.

Stevie watched them, wondering how they would react when they heard Patricia's plan. An anxious knot grew in her stomach. Did they have enough confidence in her ability to lead them, even temporarily, in their new lives?

"We're missing Dylan." Patricia scanned the room. "Is he coming?"

Lexi nodded. "He said he'd be here."

When a sharp knock rattled the front door, Stevie shot a wary glance at Lexi.

Lexi took the hint and stood up. "I'll get it."

Stevie bristled when Lexi led Dylan into the living room. There was too much at stake to worry about their shattered relationship now. As long as he behaved himself, they could work together for the sake of the coven. She'd have to find a way to be civil to him, but she had no intention of being any friendlier than necessary.

Dylan didn't even glance in Stevie's direction as he crossed the room. Without a word, he settled in on the sofa next to Deborah. He didn't bother to say hello to anyone.

So, he's going to be a jerk to everyone. She let out a soft sigh, grateful that Charlie wasn't present to see this.

Patricia pursed her lips. "Good to have you back with us, Dylan. Your trip to Africa went well, I trust?"

"It was fine." He plucked a piece of lint from his dress pants, studied it for a moment, and let it fall to the floor.

Patricia paused, studying Dylan with a quizzical expression, before she peered at Stevie with raised eyebrows.

Stevie shrugged. Dylan wasn't her problem anymore. Unless, of course, Patricia commanded him to leave Beaufort with her. Then he'd always be her problem in one way or another.

Patricia cleared her throat and squared her shoulders. "We're here tonight to address the issue of our evacuation of Beaufort. In just one day, we had a chaplain speak out against us, inciting at least part of a church congregation during the Sunday morning service. Shortly after that, Stevie and Lexi encountered a hostile environment at Backstreet Pub. On top of that, both Stevie and Dylan had their homes vandalized. It's clear the situation is escalating rapidly."

Deep creases ran across Lexi's forehead. "Don't forget, the chaplain is a witch too."

"Yes, and that complicates matters significantly." Patricia's expression hardened. "For some reason, this man has chosen to betray his own kind."

Deborah cleared her throat. "I've searched the genealogies, and I can find no intersection of the Parris family with any of our Beaufort families. He's not one of ours."

"There are plenty of other witches out there. In our travels throughout history, it wasn't unusual for some to stay behind while others fled the witch hunts." Patricia tapped a finger on the arm of her chair. "He must be a descendant from another group. He might even be related to someone who was part of Lucia's group. She had a large number of witches in her care after she sent Charlotte, Hannah, and Catherine away with Blackbeard."

Alice tilted her head. "Now that we know he's a witch, what does that mean for us? What can he do with the amulet?"

Patricia clasped her hands together. "Anything he wants."

The room fell silent, and Stevie sunk back in her chair. "Then how can you get it back from him?" If the chaplain had become all-powerful while in possession of the amulet, her mother may never be able to retrieve it.

Patricia shook her head. "I honestly don't know yet, but that isn't our most urgent matter. Right now, we have to decide where to relocate."

"I think we should head south to Wilmington." Lexi shifted in her seat. "It's a larger city, and it's on the water. We'll be able to blend in better there."

"That's too close." Ruth scowled. "How about we head even farther south? We could go to Boca Raton. Everyone I know is retiring down there."

"I'd like to stay in North Carolina. If that's possible." Randy's voice wavered as he stole a glance at Ruth. "Maybe we could go north to Hatteras?"

A sudden crash of shattering glass echoed from the dining room. Stevie bolted out of her chair and raced toward the source of the noise. The rest of the coven hustled behind her.

When Stevie reached the dining room, she gasped at a gaping hole in the front window. Stunned, she let her gaze drift to the floor, where she found a brick amid the scattered shards of glass. She bent down to pick it up.

"Step back, Stevie. I'll fix it for you." Lexi raised her hand, turning her palm toward the broken glass.

"Don't!" Patricia grabbed Lexi's arm and shoved it down. "I don't see anyone out there, but it's possible that whoever did this may be watching."

Alice covered her face with her hands. "Who would do such a thing?"

Stevie rolled the brick over, studying each side. "Mom." Her voice quaked. "Look." She passed the brick to her mother.

Patricia examined it and then held it out for all to see.

Angry red letters glared at them.

WE KNOW WHAT YOU ARE.

Chapter forty-two

Stevie

The heat rose in Stevie's cheeks as she stomped into her laundry room. She threw open a cabinet door and, with trembling hands, snatched a roll of tape from the shelf. She slammed the door closed and ground her teeth.

I have to stay calm. Stevie drew in a deep breath, but it did little to quell her anger. It was inconceivable to her that so many people, people she loved dearly, would have to abandon their homes. She and Lexi would have to give up their store. Charlie would have to leave his dad. They all had to sacrifice their comfortable lives just to accommodate hate and ignorance.

And violence. She cringed at the thought of her broken window, wondering what else the vandal might be capable of. The sound of the others shuffling back into the living room jarred her from her thoughts. She snapped up a plastic bag from a bin next to her washing machine and trudged back down the hall.

Taking care not to step on the glass shards, she kept an eye on the floor only to find that someone had already cleaned up the mess. But the jagged hole in the window remained. She positioned the plastic bag on the window and began to tape it in place.

Her mother's voice carried across the foyer. "You all need to go right away. Head out of town and find a hotel for the night. You can finish making your plans in the morning."

So this is it. It wasn't even safe to stay long enough to finish their meeting. Hatred wins. She tossed the roll of tape onto the table and made her way to the living room. Catching a movement out of the corner of her eye, she raised her head to see Charlie sitting at the top of the steps.

Stevie stared at him, wide-eyed. How long had he been there? How much had he overheard? She climbed the stairs to join him.

"Charlie, we have to go out of town tonight. We're going to stay in a hotel."

The boy looked at his feet.

Patricia's voice carried all the way up the staircase. "You will all go with Stevie. I'll stay behind to retrieve the amulet."

Stevie settled in next to Charlie and wrapped her arm around his narrow shoulders. "Everything will be all right."

"Stay together and support Stevie as you have supported me."

Stevie pulled Charlie close. "It doesn't matter where we are as long as we're together."

"She will lead the coven in my absence. Obey her." Patricia paused. "She will keep you safe."

"I'll keep you safe, Charlie," Stevie whispered.

When Patricia finished giving her directives, comments from the coven members rose up from the living room. Stevie heard no dissention, only concern for Patricia. Her determination to retrieve the amulet left her in a dangerous position, and they all knew it.

"I have to go back down there." Stevie patted Charlie's knee. "Do you want to come with me?"

Charlie nodded and followed her down the steps. The conversation in the living room had shifted to more practical matters as the coven members decided to go back to their own homes to gather their things. They agreed to meet again at Stevie's house in an hour, ready to leave town.

Ruth's brow furrowed. "We'll have to find a pet-friendly hotel. I'm not going anywhere without Patsy and Gus."

"I'm sure that won't be a problem." Randy stroked her arm.

Deborah peered at Stevie with red, puffy eyes. "Honey." She stepped closer to Stevie. "Don't mistake these tears as a sign that I lack confidence in you. Nothing could be further from the truth. I know you'll make us all proud." She sniffled and wiped away a fresh tear. "I'm crying for all of us, for the sacrifices we all make tonight. I'll miss this town terribly."

"Me too." Stevie squeezed Deborah's hand.

Charlie stood by Stevie's side as they watched the coven members prepare to leave. Each stopped to embrace Patricia as they said their goodbyes. But Dylan remained seated on the sofa, emotionless. Stevie pursed her lips and walked toward him. Charlie followed her.

Stevie stood with her back straight and her arms at her sides in forced nonchalance. "Are you planning to go with us, Dylan?"

A fresh flush of anger burned on her cheeks as he regarded her with an icy glare and ignored Charlie. She stared down at her son. This was exactly the behavior she'd hoped to spare him from.

"I'm not going with you." Dylan smirked. "I'll probably just go back to London."

Stevie stifled a relieved sigh. "Okay." She spun on her heels and crossed the room to stand with her mother. Charlie remained at her side. Ruth and Randy, having already said their goodbyes to Patricia, neared the front door while Deborah, Lexi, and Alice lingered close by. Though time was running short, no one seemed to be in a great hurry to leave.

A low murmur of voices outside caught Stevie's attention. She dashed to the window to see what was going on and pulled the curtain open just enough to peek through. A crowd of people, at least thirty men and women, now stood in front of her house. They had gathered en masse just beyond her fence. Much of the crowd spilled out onto Front Street.

Some carried lit torches with flames as menacing as the sneers on their faces. Others carried flashlights whose beams sliced through the darkness, bouncing in haphazard flashes as the crowd pressed closer to her picket fence.

"Mom!" Stevie whipped around. "Come here."

Patricia rushed to her side and peered out at the mob. Without a word, she snapped the curtains closed and grabbed Stevie's arm, yanking her away from the window.

"What should we do?" Stevie's voice pitched with urgency. She glanced down at Charlie and swallowed a lump in her throat.

"First, we stay calm." Patricia whispered so only Stevie could hear before she turned to face the other members of the coven. She pressed her lips into a thin line. "It seems we have waited too long." Following her own advice, she showed no trace of panic.

Ruth approached the window and shoved the curtain aside. "Torches!" She shook her head in disdain. "Why on earth would they be holding torches out there? Are they hunting Frankenstein?"

Stevie pulled Charlie close to her and kept her hand on his shoulder. "Let's just call the police." Fighting the swell of anxiety within her, she forced her voice to stay steady. "They'll put a stop to this madness."

"Good idea." Dylan gave a deep nod.

Stevie's lip twitched at the sound of his voice. Since he'd been so disinterested throughout the events of the evening, she was surprised to hear him chime in at all.

She pulled her cell phone from her back pocket and dialed 9-1-1. Nothing happened. She eyed her screen and sighed. "No signal. Can someone else try?"

Randy pulled out his phone and stared down at it. "No signal here either."

Patricia, Lexi, Ruth, Deborah, Alice, and Dylan all followed suit, with the same results.

"Let me try the landline." Stevie darted out of the living room to the kitchen and grabbed the cordless phone. No dial tone. She ran a shaky hand through her hair and stared toward the window over the sink. Two orange torch flames bobbed in the darkness outside.

She hurried back to the living room. "The landline is dead too."

"That can't be a coincidence." Patricia shook her head.

"I saw some of them in the backyard." Stevie's voice cracked. "We're surrounded."

She exchanged a wary glance with her mother.

"I can send out a call to the dogs." Ruth raised her eyebrows. "I'll get all of the strays to come. They can chase this crowd away."

Patricia nodded. "It's worth a try."

Ruth bowed her head in concentration and closed her eyes for a moment. "Okay. They should be here soon. They'll try to scare the crowd away without biting, if they can avoid it. But I gave them my permission to defend themselves if they have to."

"You know, that group is big and loud." Alice peered through the opening in the curtain. "It won't be long before a neighbor calls the police or a patrol car drives by and sees them."

Randy rubbed his chin. "Alice has a point. There are still plenty of good people left in this town. I think we can just ride this out."

Charlie zipped past Stevie and threw open the curtain panels.

"No, Charlie!" Stevie rushed forward and pulled him away as fast as she could. "Stay away from the windows." She spun him around and knelt down to face him. "Don't be scared. We'll find a way out of here."

"Magic."

Stevie stroked his hair. "We can't use our magic right now. If they see us use it, there will be even more trouble."

"Magic." He repeated the word louder.

Patricia rested her hand on his shoulder. "Your mother is right, Charlie. We can't use magic to stop them."

Charlie's face flushed, and he began to wail in a high-pitched, soul-piercing shriek.

Stevie gripped his arms. "Charlie, please don't do this. Not now." The words tumbled from her mouth even though she knew they were useless. He had no more control over this than she did.

Charlie screamed again and again as Stevie picked him up and carried him to the corner of the room. She sat with her back against the wall and pulled him down into her lap. He banged his head against her shoulder as she wrapped her arms around his chest. She pressed him close against her body in an effort to minimize his range of motion.

She might not know how to stop an angry mob bent on destroying her and everyone she cared about, but she knew how to keep Charlie from hurting himself. She closed her eyes, taking each slam of his head in silence.

Charlie let out a fresh wail. Stevie rocked back and forth, doubling her efforts to soothe him.

Patricia stood beside her. "Is there anything I can do?"

Stevie raised her head and saw the tears in her mother's eyes. She shook her head.

"It's getting louder out there." Alice wrung her hands. "Is the crowd getting bigger?"

Ruth stole a glance through the window. "No. They're moving *closer*." She backed away and turned to face her fellow coven members. "They've come through the gate. They're in the yard now."

Alice's mouth fell slack. "What if the police don't come in time?"

No one answered.

Charlie's shrieks shifted to moans as he rocked. "Magic."

As he settled down, Stevie loosened her grip on him. He'd never spoken the word as a suggestion before. "It's a good idea, Charlie. But we just can't use our magic right now."

Charlie whimpered and rocked faster. Fearing he would start screaming again, she cast a desperate stare at Dylan. But his focus was fixed on the window. She lowered her mental shield.

You're the only one who can read Charlie's mind. Please help him. What is he trying to tell me?

Nothing. Dylan didn't even spare a glance in her direction.

With a defeated sigh, she raised her mental shield once more.

The voices outside rumbled closer and the glow from the torches grew brighter as the mob pressed in toward the house.

Chapter forty-three

Stevie

Stevie kept her arms tight around Charlie as she rocked him. Tears streamed down the boy's cheeks as he chanted one word, his only word, over and over again.

"Magic, magic, magic…"

His moans faded to sporadic whimpers, but his body remained rigid. Stevie had been through this enough times to know he wasn't finished yet. She had to stay with him and keep him calm. She ignored the soreness in her shoulder as he pressed his head against it.

"I'm so sorry that this has happened. It's all my fault for inviting that chaplain to speak at my church." Despair brimmed in Alice's eyes as she wrung her hands. "I…I just can't believe they're doing this."

"I have an idea!" Lexi pointed a finger in the air. "What if we confuse them? We could make them see something that isn't there, just long enough for us to get out of here."

"Like a mirage?" Alice sniffled and dried her tears with a crumpled tissue.

"We could make them perceive no movement from the house even as we walk right out through the door?" Deborah's eyes brightened with hope. "Excellent idea, Lexi."

"That's big magic." Randy shook his head, dubious. "Can we possibly fool that many people at once?"

"All of our powers combined aren't enough to work a spell that strong." Patricia stood with her hands on her hips. "We can't do it without the amulet."

"Magic!" Charlie slammed his head against Stevie's shoulder. "Magic!"

"Shh." Stevie tightened her hold on him.

"The dogs should be here by now. I wonder what's taking them so long." Ruth squinted through the gap in the curtains. "What the hell?" She jerked back. "The dogs are out there, sitting across the street. Why aren't they barking?"

"Try sending them another message." Patricia crossed her arms and waited.

Ruth closed her eyes for a moment and then looked through the window. "They're just sitting over there like a bunch of dummies. They aren't interested in the crowd all. I'm not close enough to be able to read them, but they should easily be able to hear me. I don't know what the problem is, but it's not working."

Patricia drew in a deep breath and let her arms fall to her sides. "Then I see only one way through this."

Stevie's breath caught in her throat as she realized that her mother intended to follow the example Diana had set in Salem. "Mom, no!" She couldn't let her sacrifice herself as a diversion. "There must be another way!"

Patricia leaned down to Stevie. "Someday, you'll understand." She patted her shoulder. "Look after your father for me."

She stood straight and squared her shoulders. "You'll have to run as soon as they take me. Don't waste a second." She strode toward the front door.

"No, I'll go." Deborah grabbed Patricia's arm.

Lexi gasped.

Patricia embraced her dearest friend. "You know why I must do this. I couldn't live with myself if you went in my place. We all have our roles to play. This is mine."

"Yes, it is." Dylan smirked. "Just like Diana and Lucia in Salem. What has happened before is happening again."

Puzzled, Randy tilted his head. "Salem? What are you talking about?"

Stevie's heart skipped a beat as she shot a glance at Patricia. Her mother's grim expression confirmed what she already knew to be true—only she, Alice, and Deborah had heard the story of Salem. She leaned in close to Charlie's ear. "I know what you're telling me. I understand now."

Charlie nodded and his rocking slowed to a stop. "Magic."

"Yes, it is." Stevie swallowed hard. "You need to go to your room now, Charlie. Stay there until I come for you. Do you understand?"

Charlie nodded and stood up.

Stevie rose with him. "Go on now." As soon as Charlie left the living room, she whirled around and faced Dylan. Overwhelmed with fury, her fists clenched as she stalked toward him.

"Stevie, wait." Patricia pulled her back.

Deborah studied Dylan with narrowed eyes. "How do *you* know about Diana?"

Alice and Deborah came to stand with Patricia and Stevie, forming a tight line.

"What's going on here?" Ruth hunched forward, scowling.

Stevie ducked as an enormous crash shattered the living room window, showering them with shards of glass. The shouts from the angry crowd outside filled the room.

"Kill the witches!"

"Burn them!"

The mob began to chant. "Burn them! Burn them!"

Patricia, Stevie, Deborah, and Alice did not flinch. Ignoring the hostile mob surrounding the house, they remained focused on Dylan.

Randy, however, began to drag the coffee table toward the open window.

"Don't bother with that, Randy. None of this is real." Patricia waved her hand in a sweeping gesture. "Ignore it."

"What?" Lexi tilted her head and glanced from Patricia to Stevie.

"That angry mob is some sort of magical hallucination. That's what Charlie was trying to tell us. And it's the reason why the dogs are sitting across the street. They're confused. There's no crowd for them to scare away." Stevie tightened her jaw in anger.

"Well, what does Dylan have to do with it?" Lexi gestured toward him, her eyes wide with confusion.

"He shouldn't know anything about what happened with Diana and Lucia in Salem. That secret resides in the amulet. Only those who have communed with the stone know the details of that night." Patricia pursed her lips. "Dylan has the amulet."

Making him the most powerful witch alive.

Chapter forty-four

Stevie

Stevie's mouth went dry. She enjoyed no sense of relief from the knowledge that her beloved town had not descended into paranoid hysteria. There hadn't even been time to marvel at Charlie's magnificent mind, which had somehow been impervious to the hallucination they'd all succumbed to. There was no joy in this moment. Only pain.

Dylan had betrayed them and tortured them with their worst fear, a terror bred into them through countless generations of persecution. He'd stolen the amulet and broken the most basic covenant of their people. She gulped. She'd invited this monster into her home. Into her bed.

Stevie stared at him in disbelief. She'd opened her heart to him and let him read her thoughts. He knew everything about her, but she had never known him at all.

Dylan met her glare. "I can't believe the kid figured it out. He's smarter than I thought."

Stevie's face hardened. She raised her hand to strike him. Her mother caught her arm and shoved it down.

Outside, the night fell silent. Flickering lights from the torches and flashlights disappeared. Scattered shards of glass popped up and found their places within the window frame as the terrors of the night erased themselves. As if nothing had happened at all.

"Why did you do this, Dylan?" Lexi's shoulders slumped. "Why did you betray us?"

Dylan's gaze shifted from Stevie to Lexi. "Because I could." His callous reply sent a chill racing up Stevie's spine.

"Why don't you just tell us what you want?" Patricia held her head high and her back straight.

"Oh, I already have what I want." Dylan eyed Patricia. "I have the amulet." A wicked sneer crossed his face.

A forceful knock shook Stevie's front door, and the knob jiggled as the person on the other side tried to open it.

"Stevie?" A male voice boomed. "Are you okay?"

Stevie sucked in a sharp breath. She recognized that voice.

No one spoke.

"I know you're in there," the familiar voice called. "I'm coming in." After a brief pause, the door burst open with a rush of magic.

The entire coven turned to face their visitor as he stormed into the house.

His soulful brown eyes, full of questions and concern, met Stevie's desperate gaze.

"Dylan." Her throat tightened at the sight of him. Here was the man she loved with all her heart. The real Dylan.

My Dylan.

I never should have doubted him.

"I just got back. Your phone—." Spotting his doppelganger, he drew back in surprise. "What the hell is going on in here?"

231

"Well, this is awkward." The other Dylan smirked. "I guess it's time for me to fess up."

The coven watched in horror as his face began to distort. His chin rounded and his eyes sunk in. His hair lightened and thinned as he shrunk a few inches in height.

It was the chaplain stood who stood before them now.

"Chaplain Parris!" Alice clamped her hand over her mouth.

"Oh, but I'm not finished yet." A mischievous grin formed on his face. "You'll have to forgive me for dragging this out. You see, I've been waiting for this moment for a very long time."

Dylan eased in beside Stevie and wrapped a protective arm around her waist.

Once again, the person who stood before them began to change. The chaplain's hair filled in and grew longer as his cheekbones rose. His eyebrows thinned and arched. His pants and button-down shirt morphed into a flowing, black dress.

Stevie's breaths came in ragged gasps as she watched the chaplain transform into a woman.

No. It can't be.

Patricia lurched forward. "Susan."

Chapter forty-five

Stevie

Stevie couldn't speak, dumbfounded by the sight of Susan standing in her living room…wearing her mother's amulet.

Dylan stiffened, and he pulled away.

Stevie raised a shaky hand to her mouth. Of all that the coven had suffered at the hands of the dark witch, he'd lost the most—his mother.

Susan's eyes darted to Dylan as he strode toward her. Flashes of white light danced on his palms.

She clucked. "You don't want to do that." She pointed a bony finger at him. "It won't end well for you."

"Dylan, stay back." Stevie's voice cracked. "She has the amulet!"

Dylan stopped in his tracks and gazed back at Stevie. Saying nothing, his face hardened with resolve, and he raised his hands toward Susan.

"No! Don't!" Stevie grabbed at him, but he ignored her pleas.

A vivid white force erupted from his palms and streaked across the room toward their enemy. But it stopped short, inches from Susan's leering face.

The muscles in Dylan's arms flexed as he propelled his energy forward, pushing with all his might. Stevie cringed. There was no way he could beat the amulet.

Susan regarded him with no more concern than if he were a newborn kitten. With a slight gesture of her fingers, she reflected the bolts of his powerful electric energy back at him.

He kept a wide stance and raised his arms to block the rebounding attack. But when his own magic struck against his hands, a burst of fiery red energy exploded from his palms and shot all the way up his arms. He stumbled back and cried out in pain.

"Dylan!" Stevie grabbed him and pulled him out of harm's way. Breathless, she shielded him from Susan, hoping to give him a chance to recover.

Patricia's hands curled into fists. "How did you get out of the hospital?"

"Well it was really quite brilliant if I do say so myself." Susan snickered. "You see, there was this chaplain. Sad and misguided fellow. Very easy to manipulate. He got the amulet for me."

Alice cleared her throat. "You're talking about him in the past tense. Is he...dead?"

"He might as well be. He now bears an unfortunate resemblance to me. He'll spend the rest of his days at the hospital." Susan glared at Patricia. "It's actually a fate worse than death. No one knows that better than I do."

Stevie blinked and remembered Randy's vision and Ruth's phone call to the hospital. It all made sense now.

Dylan bristled as Susan gloated about her escape, poised as if he might lunge for her at any moment. Stevie knew that would be a fatal mistake on his part. Susan wouldn't tolerate two attacks, nor did she have to. The balance of power was in her favor now.

Stevie lowered her mental shield and allowed Dylan access to her thoughts.

Stay calm. Please.

Dylan gave an almost imperceptible nod, but his chest continued to heave with angry, rapid breaths. Stevie couldn't blame him; she wanted to attack as much as he did. She stole a quick glance at the other coven members. All of them, even the old ones, stood with balled fists and clenched teeth, just like her.

"I'm the one who led the church service yesterday. Wasn't that marvelous?" She rested her hand on her chest. "Perhaps I missed my calling."

"Why would you tell others about us?" Alice cocked her head. "Why would you create unnecessary fear?"

"Oh, but I didn't tell anyone about you. Much like the show you saw tonight." She gestured toward the window. "It was all a hallucination designed just for you." Susan grinned. "The other parishioners experienced a different sermon altogether." Her gaze fell on Stevie. "Same thing with Backstreet and your walk home."

Stevie fought hard not to wither under the weight of Susan's glare. She kept her face immutable. No anger. No fear. She didn't bother to ask about the vandalism on her front door. She knew who was responsible. Their secret was still safe, even if they weren't.

"What do you want, Susan?" Wrath clipped Patricia's words.

Susan snapped her head in Patricia's direction. "For twelve years, I wasted away in that psych ward. Twelve miserable years. And every single day, I dreamed of this." She licked her lips. "Your day of reckoning has finally come."

Stevie cast an uneasy glance at her mother.

Susan spread her arms in a gesture that encompassed the entire coven. "You make these fools kneel down before you. But you've never deserved that honor."

"I've never asked anyone to kneel." Patricia raised her chin.

"It's true; she hasn't." Alice clasped her hands together. "But we certainly have, and we'll do it again. She is our queen."

Declarations of agreement rose up from all the coven members.

"Shut up!" Susan shrieked and then snapped her mouth closed. She took in a deep breath before she spoke again. "I'm still talking."

Alice gasped. Ruth let out a low growl that would have sent every dog in Beaufort slinking away with its tail between its legs. Stevie dug her nails into her palms as her own anger boiled up within her.

"There can only be *one* queen." Susan held her head high, as though she were addressing an auditorium instead of a living room. "If you won't follow me, then I *will* destroy you."

"It doesn't have to be this way, Susan." Patricia maintained her composure, defying the tension in the room. "No one has to get hurt. Let the coven leave so you and I can discuss this alone."

Stevie winced. She couldn't leave her peace-loving mother alone with the dark witch. Susan would end her life without batting an eye.

"The fact is, Patricia, your opinion doesn't matter anymore. I have the amulet." The corners of her mouth curled up in a self-satisfied grin as she cupped the amethyst in her hand. "*I* am the queen now."

"Patricia is our queen with or without the amulet." Deborah's expression crumpled in contempt. "*She* has earned our respect."

Randy cleared his throat. "Most of the witches in this town don't even know the amulet still exists. They've chosen Lucia's line for leadership out of respect, not out of fear of the amulet's power."

Susan's face twisted with a growing rage. "You will all kneel down before me. I am your queen now!" Her lip twitched. "Kneel!"

No one flinched. No one moved. Not a single coven member obeyed her command. Stevie stood firm. This wasn't a fight she was willing to run from.

At the sight of their defiance, Susan's face grew red with fury. She stalked toward Patricia with a scornful glare.

Without warning, Dylan jumped in front of Patricia, shielding her.

Stevie's stomach clenched in panic. What had he heard?

A glowing crimson light emerged from the centers of Susan's hands. She held her arms out in front of her, her sight set on Dylan.

Patricia tried to step around him, but he blocked her.

The light pulsed and exploded out from Susan's palms. Stevie lunged forward, but she was too late. The dark witch's magic slammed straight into Dylan. He dropped to the floor with a thud.

Susan sneered down at him. "You just don't learn, do you?"

Randy stooped next to Dylan. Stevie froze, wanting to help but unable to leave her mother's side. When Dylan's eyes flickered open, she let out the breath she'd been holding and faced his attacker once more.

Patricia held up her hands. "Please. Let the others go. It's me you want."

"No. I want witnesses," Susan hissed. "They need to watch you die." The vile red hue of her power stained her palms once again. She raised her right arm as she focused squarely on Patricia.

Stevie hunched forward and drew all of her power from her core. Prickly jolts of electric force raced through her body and into her palms. She raised both hands and blasted everything she had at Susan's torso.

Patricia did the same, concentrating her magic in the same area Stevie targeted. Lexi, Ruth, Deborah, and Alice joined in as well, each sending white streaks soaring across the living room. The bright light produced by Stevie and Patricia dwarfed the threads of power coming from the other coven members.

But Susan didn't falter as they launched their attack. She swatted the bolts of magical force away as if they were nothing more than annoying houseflies.

Stevie held nothing back. She fired again and again, to no avail. Susan remained unscathed.

We can't go on like this forever. Stevie sent another powerful blast. *We'll all collapse from exhaustion…then she'll kill Mom anyway.*

There had to be some way to take her advantage away. She studied Susan, watching her dispassionate defensive swats. She handled each one with ease.

As the others continued to relentlessly fire on Susan, focusing their magic toward her heart, Stevie shifted her aim. Her gaze dipped downward. She lowered her arms and fired two power-ful bolts of lightning at Susan's feet.

Susan shouted in surprise as she lost her balance and fell to the floor, landing hard on her side. Stevie raced toward her, hoping to snatch the amethyst necklace before the dark witch had the opportunity to recover from the shock of the fall.

The coven halted their attack, giving Stevie a chance to get close to Susan. She'd almost reached the dark witch's toppled body when a fiery pain shot through her rib cage. She stumbled back as her legs wobbled beneath her, threatening to give way in the wake of the blow. She never saw it coming.

"Leave her alone!" Patricia demanded. She began to fire on Susan again. Without hesitation, Lexi, Deborah, Ruth, and Alice joined in the effort.

Stevie gasped for air as the coven continued the fight without her. She watched the dark witch deflect the coven's attack with ease. Even collapsed on the floor, Susan managed to out-maneuver each strike. As the pain in Stevie's ribcage began to subside, she steadied herself and added her own magic to the assault once more.

With a feral growl, Susan rose to her feet. She locked her glare on Patricia as she continued to deflect the coven's magic. "There can only be one queen!"

She stopped swatting the magic that soared her way, taking each strike with little more than an uneasy flinch. She uncurled her fist and produced another blast of red light. Streaks of black roiled within the throbbing ball of energy.

Stevie's stomach twisted at the sight. "No!"

Susan eyed Stevie and gave her a chilling wink before she shifted her gaze back to Patricia. She drew her arm back and hurled the pulsating ball of malevolent energy straight into Patricia's chest.

Patricia soared across the room and slammed flat against the wall. Stevie clamped her hand over her mouth, stifling a scream, as she watched her mother slip down and slump onto the floor.

Randy helped Dylan to his feet and then rushed to Patricia's side.

Stevie couldn't draw a single breath as she watched Randy examine her mother. His face was grim. "Mom?" Hot tears welled in her eyes.

Randy rested his hand on Patricia's forehead for a moment. Her eyes were open but unfocused. She had the same vacant stare that Charlie had displayed during his seizure.

"Can you heal her?" Stevie's voice hitched.

Tears pooled in Randy's eyes as he glanced up to meet Stevie's desperate gaze. "I'm sorry." He swept his hand downward and closed Patricia's eyes forever.

"No!" Stevie dropped to her knees. "No!" She grabbed her mother's shoulders and shook them. "Mom! Mom, come back!"

"She's gone, honey." Randy spoke with a gentle stillness.

"We *have* to do something!" With trembling hands, she cupped Patricia's face. "Try CPR!"

Randy shook his head. "It's too late. It won't work. Her brain is already dead. Susan made sure of that." Disgust dripped from his words as he glared at the evil witch who stood on the other side of the room.

Stevie gazed down at her mother's still body and sank back on her heels. She couldn't hold back her anguished tears as a lifetime of memories raced through her mind. Smiles and laughter. Kissed boo-boos. Hugs in times of trouble. Advice in times of uncertainty. Constant, unwavering love. *Mom...how can I go on without you?*

She'd been Stevie's rock. Her peace in the storm.

Peace. Patricia and all of the queens before her had sought peace for their people. Never did they use their powers against those who tried to harm them. They simply ran.

But they'd never encountered anyone like Susan before. It had been a mistake to let this dark witch live, even tucked away in a hospital. Stevie gulped. Patricia had paid for that mistake with her life.

Stevie slowly rose to her feet and faced Susan, whose smug grin mocked the unimaginable pain of her loss.

There will be no peace as long as the dark witch lives. Stevie knew what she had to do.

"Stevie, don't!" Dylan reached for her arm, just missing her as she zipped past him on her way to Susan.

Stevie raised her arms in front of her body. Her hands twisted into claws. Electric magic and fiery rage meshed as one uncontrollable force inside her. It burned in her veins as she pushed her growing power from the center of her body and down through her arms toward her hands.

Powered by grief and a fury Stevie had never experienced before, the magic within her burst forth as a blinding white light. It fired from her palms toward Susan.

Susan threw her head back and laughed before she disappeared, leaving nothing but thin air in her place.

The destructive force Stevie had created exploded through the empty space Susan had occupied only a second earlier. With its intended target out of the way, it slammed into the wall, blasting a hole several feet wide. The entire room shuddered, tossing framed pictures to the floor in a squall of shattered glass and splintered wood.

Cool night air blew in through the jagged opening in the living room. Stevie stared out into the darkness with her back to the rest of the grieving coven members.

She couldn't bring herself to look back just yet.

Refusing to think about what she'd say to Charlie and her father, Stevie wasn't ready to face the reality of her mother's death. She wanted only to feel nothing.

But a new sensation commanded her attention.

The knot in her stomach transformed into a strange flutter. A quickening. She pressed her hand to her belly, imagining a small butterfly whose wings generated warmth as he moved within her. The heat spread out from her core, filling her heart and mind. A wave of peace washed over her, bathing her in serenity. She closed her eyes, relishing the sensation.

She raised her hand to her heart, overcome with a sudden, all-encompassing love. It was a love as big as a mother's devotion to her child and as strong as the bond between sisters.

More tears rolled down her cheeks, but she made no effort to wipe them away.

Stevie reveled for just a moment in the flood of warmth, overwhelmed by enormous devotion for her people and their history. She didn't think about what had happened or what was to come. She only experienced the wonder of her transformation.

The four elements of magic welcomed her into the fold. She'd seen them all represented by the candles her mother used on the night of Vanessa's binding ritual.

The air element came to her in the form of a cool breeze, brushing her cheek with a welcoming kiss. It carried with it the scent of green grass, which swayed in the wind on the other side of the hole in the wall. As soon as she recognized this as the earth element, she heard the soft lull of the low waves on Taylor's Creek. Water had made itself known. Only one element remained.

Fire.

Stevie remained still and watchful, waiting for the last element to welcome her. All of her senses were on alert. Where was fire?

The answer came to her with a sensation that was far too bold and intense to ignore. Fire had arrived.

Within her.

What had begun as a warmth in her core now burned hot in the form of fierce determination. She dropped her arms to her sides and raised her chin. Her destiny was clear—a humbling honor, both joyful and terrifying. She drank it all in amidst her crushing heartbreak, savoring this unexpected switch triggered by genetics and magic.

Stevie had become a queen.

And she had work to do. She'd have to find a way to pick up the pieces of Susan's destruction and decide a course of action. Swiping her hands across her face, she dried her tears before she drew in a great breath and turned to face her coven.

Stevie gasped at the sight before her. Her gaze traveled along the line of coven members: Ruth, Randy, Deborah, Lexi, Alice, and Dylan. Every single one of them knelt before her. Now, they honored her with bowed heads.

The weight of her mother's burden sank upon her shoulders. As she gazed upon her loyal coven members another great burst of love ripped through her. A love so deep and wide, it was irrevocably woven into her soul.

Dylan raised his head first, his eyes bright with awe. Stevie met his gaze and realized that she'd left her mental shield down. He knew what had happened to her. He'd witnessed her pain as well as her euphoria. He knew she'd become a very different person than she'd been only moments before.

There were no words sufficient for this moment. She nodded, acknowledging Dylan and all of the others.

Dylan stood and offered his hand to Alice. He helped her to her feet while the others rose as well.

Stevie stared past them at her mother's body. Someone had smoothed her dress and positioned her arms at her sides. The coven members looked at Stevie with reverence and expectation.

She bit down on her lip, unable to speak.

Deborah's tears fell unabated. "Stevie, should we continue with our plan to leave Beaufort?"

The coven members awaited her response in silence. A long moment passed as Stevie, realizing that she alone held the responsibility for the future of her people, considered her options.

A soft creak came from the stairs.

Charlie!

Stevie assumed Charlie had been called to action by the cacophony of sadness he must have sensed coming from this room. She suspected that her son sought to quell the emotional pain of others just like a firefighter sought to rescue innocents from a blaze.

Stevie stepped toward the doorway, hoping to block Charlie's entrance and prevent him from seeing Patricia's body. She heard another creak as he neared the bottom of the steps.

As she crossed the room, she realized that she had not answered Deborah's question. She spun around to face the coven once more.

She held her head high. "No. We're staying. We're going to take back our amulet."

Chapter forty-six

Stevie

Stevie met Charlie at the foot of the stairs, and the bliss of her transition into queen slipped away as a memory. Her heart grew heavy with the weight of Patricia's death. She had no idea how to tell him that his grandmother was gone.

"Charlie, sit with me." She sat down on the third stair and patted the empty space next to her. "I have to tell you something."

Stevie watched as her young son climbed the steps to meet her. He furrowed his brow, and she wondered how much he already knew.

"Grandma is gone, Charlie." She hated the abruptness of her own words, but she saw no value in dragging it out.

He offered no reaction to her revelation.

In the silence that fell between them, she heard a bustle of activity coming from the living room.

Deborah's voice carried into the foyer. "Dylan and Lexi, please repair the hole in the wall. And Randy, would you take care of the window in the dining room?"

Stevie heard the crunch of broken glass beneath a shoe.

Deborah sniffed. "Ruth and Alice, can you two help me with the knickknacks and pictures. Let's put everything right before Stevie comes back."

Stevie raked her hands through her hair. *They can't fix everything.*

Realizing that Charlie might have misunderstood her words, she curled her arm around him. In his literal mind, "Grandma is gone" might mean nothing more than she'd returned to her own home. He may very well think that he would see her again tomorrow. She blinked back the fresh tears that pooled in her eyes.

She decided to try again. She'd have to be as direct as possible if there was any chance of Charlie understanding what had happened.

She inhaled a deep breath knowing the words she intended to speak next would split her heart in two. "Grandma *died* tonight." She blinked again, struggling to keep her own sadness at bay. "Do you understand what that means?"

Charlie offered no reaction.

Stevie sighed in frustration. How could he know what that meant? He'd never lost anyone before.

She didn't know if heaven really existed, but it was a comforting thought in light of her mother's death. Maybe that concept would help Charlie come to terms with his grandmother's absence. "She's in heaven now. We won't see her here again. She's gone. Do you understand?"

Stevie had run out of ways to explain death to her five-year-old son. She didn't know what she would do if he didn't get it this time. Her stomach twisted in knots as she awaited his response.

After an agonizing moment, he nodded.

Telling Charlie about Patricia brought the loss to the forefront of her mind in a rush of grief. It was real now. There was no going back. She'd never see her mother again. She sniffed and swiped her hands across her wet cheeks.

"I'm sad. Everyone who knew Grandma will be sad too. If you feel sad, that's okay. It's totally normal. I'll be here for you."

Charlie reached for her, but Stevie raised her hand to block him. "I know what you can do." She lowered his arm between them. "I know you want to take my sadness away, but you can't. Not yet. I *need* to feel this. I can't explain it. I just know that I have to go through this." She wrapped her arms around him.

Randy emerged from the living room with his cell phone in his hand. "I'm sorry to interrupt." He grimaced. "The phone service is back up. I really can't wait much longer to make the call. Are you ready?"

Stevie swallowed hard and nodded.

Chapter forty-seven

Stevie

Later that night, Stevie parked her Prius in front of her house and made her way up the walkway to her porch. She climbed the steps slower than usual, weighed down with grief and the burden of her new responsibility.

A knot of emotion welled in her raw throat. Telling her dad that his beloved wife had died was the hardest thing she'd ever done. In her whole life, she'd never seen him cry—and it had been gut-wrenching to watch it happen. *I don't know how we can ever heal from this loss.*

Determined to help her father, she'd started by sparing him the truth of Patricia's death. She closed her eyes, remembering how they'd covered up her murder. Lexi, Deborah, and Ruth had shuffled out of the house before the funeral home employees came to take her mother's body. Randy had taken care of all the paperwork, citing the official cause of death as a stroke. When Dylan and Alice volunteered to stay with Charlie, she'd left for her father's house. It had all happened so fast.

Just before she reached the door, a movement in the shadows caught her eye. She spun around to face the source of the disturbance and raised her arms, ready to defend herself.

"Who's there?" She squinted into the darkness.

"I'm sorry for your loss," the familiar voice replied. "I tried to warn you."

"You could have told me that your psychotic mother had come back." Stevie ground her teeth. "Come out so I can see you."

Vanessa crept out of the shadows. Her hood provided cover for her scars, but the bold green hue of her eyes still peeked out. "How's Charlie handling this?"

"That is *none* of your business." Stevie kept her palms forward, ready to strike. If Vanessa took one wrong step, she'd blow her to pieces.

"It wasn't real, you know. Backstreet Pub, the paint on your door, the people on the street…it was all a forced hallucination." She glanced back toward the docks before returning her gaze to Stevie. "Even the sermon at the church. The rest of the congregation watched her deliver a regular sermon that she'd copied from a television minister. You, Alice, and Lexi were the only ones who experienced the witch hysteria."

"I know all of that. Your crazy mother made sure to take credit for her activities." Stevie sneered. "We know we don't have to worry about witch hunts breaking out anytime soon."

Vanessa raised her head, revealing some of the scarring along her jawline. "You need to worry about what my mother will do next if you stay." Again, she glanced toward the docks, teetering in place like a nervous cat. "It's only going to get worse."

"Our days of peaceful self-preservation are over." Stevie clenched her fists. "We are prepared to fight."

Vanessa's chin dropped, draping her damaged face in darkness once more. "You can't possibly win this battle."

Stevie narrowed her eyes at this vulnerable version of Vanessa. She bore little resemblance to the formidable woman she'd once been. She shook away the thought. Whatever brought Vanessa to her doorstep was of little matter. If the dark witch was enduring some sort of crisis of conscience, Stevie had no sympathy for her. Not now.

"Go away." She let herself into her house. "I have a funeral to plan."

Stevie closed the door behind her and locked it. She began to cross the foyer but stopped mid-step. Her gaze flicked to the portrait of Hannah, Catherine, and Charlotte on the wall. She was drawn to it, connected in a way that she'd never experienced before. She eased closer and examined the faces of the original Beaufort witches.

Before this night, she'd admired the painting for its simple beauty and its connection to her history. But now, as she gazed into Charlotte's painted eyes, she experienced the portrait on a different level. For in her ancestor's expression, Stevie saw all that echoed in her own soul—love and loss, determination and responsibility. She'd never noticed that before.

The painting hadn't changed; Stevie was sure of that. The change had come from within her, the moment her mother died. The moment she became queen. Grief pricked her heart once again, and she clutched at her chest like she could hold it all in. A silent scream of agony escaped her lips, and she clamped her hand against the wall to keep from doubling over.

"How did it go, dear?" Alice ambled in from the kitchen carrying an empty basket in her right hand. "Should I go check on your father?"

Stevie straightened her back and cleared her throat. Glimpsing the dark circles under Alice's eyes, she shook her head. "No. Thanks though. He said he wanted to be alone. I'll go back over there first thing in the morning."

Alice nodded. "I made you a sandwich. It's on the counter. I also left some packets of tea for you. It's a special blend of mine. It'll help you relax."

"Thanks, Alice." Stevie doubted that there was anything strong enough to help her relax right now. "It's late. You need to get some rest yourself. Let me drive you home."

"Not to worry, dear. Randy is coming back to pick me up. He should be here any minute." She shifted the basket to her left hand. "I'm going to leave this basket on your front porch tonight. Be sure to check on it regularly in the coming days."

Stevie arched her eyebrow. "What's the basket for?"

"Word of the queen's—I mean your mother's—passing will travel quickly. The other witches in town will leave gifts for you."

"To honor my mother?"

"Well, yes, but also to show their allegiance to you." Alice gave her a thin smile. "The ascension of a new queen is no small matter for us."

Queen. Stevie didn't think she'd ever get used to hearing that word tossed around. It didn't fit her at all. But it had suited her mother well. A new lump formed in her throat. She hadn't even had the opportunity to comprehend the full scope of her mother's role as the leader of their people, and now that responsibility rested on her own shoulders.

Alice patted her arm. "It will be okay, dear. You'll have all the help you need."

A movement at the top of the stairs caught Stevie's attention. Her gaze traveled upward to see who was there.

"Hey, Stevie." Dylan waved to her from the second floor landing.

Her heart leap at the sight of him. They hadn't had a moment alone since he'd come back from Africa. She had so much to tell him, but more than anything, she just wanted his arms wrapped around her again.

The rumble of Randy's old Buick bellowed from outside. Alice waved. "Good night, dear. Call me if you need anything."

"I will. Thanks." She closed the door behind the older woman.

"Charlie's asleep." Dylan made his way down the steps. Stevie held her breath as he approached, anticipating his embrace.

He raised his hand and brushed a stray hair from her cheek. She closed her eyes, drinking in the gentleness of his touch.

When she opened her eyes again, her gaze met Dylan's. The corners of his mouth drew up in a bitter sneer, and without warning, he threw her against the door.

The air rushed out of her lungs, leaving her breathless. She couldn't scream. In an instant, he clasped his large hand on her neck, pinning her against the door. She clawed at him, trying with all of her might to undo the grip he had on her. But it was useless. The more she struggled, the harder he squeezed. He said nothing as he watched her terror with wide-eyed delight.

Stevie couldn't breathe.

Dylan's face and body began to change, morphing into the image of Susan. The dark witch bared her teeth as she tightened her deadly grip on Stevie's throat, crushing her windpipe.

"This is a reminder that I can get to you anytime, anywhere." Susan wagged a finger in Stevie's face. "And there's not a damn thing you can do about it."

Dark spots gathered and grew, obscuring Stevie's vision. She began to slip away.

"I am the queen now! Remember that!" All of a sudden, Susan disappeared, and the pressure on Stevie's airway relieved. She dropped to her knees and gasped for a breath, coughing and sputtering as she tried to collect herself.

Charlie! Her gaze darted to the second floor landing. She leapt forward and raced up the stairs to his bedroom. Still dizzy, she threw the door open and stared into the dark expanse of his room. Her hand fumbled against the wall until she found the switch and flipped on the light.

Charlie was in his bed, sound asleep, and Dylan dozed in the chair next to him. They were fine, both of them. Stevie slumped against the wall.

Dylan stirred and opened his eyes. "Stevie, what's wrong?"

Stevie gestured for Dylan to follow her as she clicked off the light in Charlie's room. She didn't want to wake him if she could avoid it. Together, they stepped out into the hallway, and she pulled the door closed with a soft click.

"You're so pale. Are you okay?" Dylan stepped closer. His eyes grew wide as he took in the sight of her. "Your neck. What happened?" He reached out to touch the angry red mark encircling her throat.

Stevie backed away as he drew near. Raising her arms, she blocked his approach. "Stay back."

Dylan frowned in confusion. "It's just me, Stevie." He lowered his hand.

She studied his face, searching for a sign, some indisputable proof that he was the real Dylan. She saw no difference between him and the beast who had just attacked her in her foyer. She lowered her mental shield.

Can you hear my thoughts?

"Of course I can." Dylan's forehead crumpled with worry.

Overcome with exhaustion, Stevie leaned against the doorframe. She would find no comfort in his arms tonight. Not after what had happened in the foyer with Susan. She shifted her gaze downward to the floor. She couldn't stand to look at him.

"Stevie, what's going on?"

She opened her mouth to speak only to stop before uttering a word. She didn't have the energy to describe what had happened. Instead, she let the memory of Susan's attack flow through her mind.

Dylan's mouth fell open. He reached for her, but she jerked back.

"We can get through this." He let his arm fall to his side. "I know we can."

Stevie raised her hands. "Just not tonight. It's all too much for me right now."

"I can't leave you and Charlie here alone. If she comes back…"

Stevie nodded. "You can take one of the guest rooms. We'll talk more another time."

Chapter forty-eight

Stevie

Stevie sat at her kitchen table with a nearly empty glass of chardonnay in front of her. She raised it to her lips and finished off the wine in one long, unceremonious gulp. It wasn't her first drink of the evening, and it wouldn't be her last.

Lexi leaned against the counter, her cheek cupped in her hand. "You can talk to me, you know. You can talk to all of us. You're not in this alone."

"I know."

Stevie traced the base of her glass with her finger. *Alone.* She hadn't had a minute to herself since her mother's death. The coven had made sure of that with staggered, incessant visits over the last couple of days. It hadn't taken her long to figure out their routine.

But Stevie wanted to be alone. Her grief for her mother was profound enough on its own, but the metamorphosis she'd undergone since Patricia's death overwhelmed her. What had started as an intense maternal love for all of the witches in Beaufort had become an almost feral need to protect them all at any cost. And with Susan on the loose, no one was safe.

255

She did not want this burden.

She touched her neck. Remembering Susan's attack, she swallowed hard. Randy had healed the deep bruises, but in her memories, she still choked under the dark witch's grasp.

Susan had declared herself queen, and she'd left no room for doubt. Stevie knew what would happen to her and her coven if she attempted to fill her mother's role.

The thought of leaving town with Charlie grew more appealing by the second.

When the doorbell rang, Stevie groaned.

Lexi wagged a finger at her. "Be nice. We're all just trying to help."

"I'll get it," Dylan called from the den.

Stevie listened in as he made his way down the hall, with Charlie's light footsteps trailing behind him. When the front door creaked open, Dylan greeted Alice.

"Is she talking yet?" Alice kept her voice low.

Dylan let out a heavy sigh. "Not to me."

Alice was quiet for a moment. "Don't worry, dear. She'll find her way. We'll get her through this."

The old, wooden floorboards of the hallway creaked as Dylan and Charlie led Alice to the kitchen.

"This is the real Alice." Dylan gave Stevie a curt nod and stepped aside to make way for the older witch.

No one entered the house without his approval. All of the coven members knew to lower their mental shield so he could access their thoughts before he'd allow them anywhere near Stevie. It was a critical component of their new magical security system. Though it provided a small comfort during a time of terrible uncertainty, Stevie knew it failed to address the real threat. They might be able to detect Susan when she came back, in whatever form she chose, but there was nothing they could do to protect themselves from her malignant power.

Alice strolled through the doorway toting the now overflowing basket she'd left on the front porch the night Patricia died. Charlie stood beside her, flapping his hands, signaling to Stevie that he also recognized their visitor as the real Alice.

Between Charlie's ability to see through magical hallucinations and Dylan's gift of mind reading, Stevie knew Susan hadn't attempted any more of her tricks in the last couple of days.

Stevie's gaze drifted upward to Dylan. His broad chest, which had once been a comfortable place to rest her head, jutted forward, tense and alert. Always on guard, he kept his back straight, ready for battle.

Her lover had become her sentinel.

She gazed into his eyes. Those warm brown irises that had always been so full of compassion were now cold and distant. She found it impossible to lose herself in the reflection of his love anymore. Instead, he'd been consumed by the same maelstrom of rage and grief that she had.

Above all, in Dylan's coldness, she sensed his desire for vengeance. She saw it in his stark glare and the rigid set of his jaw. She recognized it easily, for the same desire burned within her as well.

"Stevie." Alice set the basket on the table. "They've been leaving offerings for you all day." She began to pull out small packets of dried herbs, colorful gemstones, handmade soaps, and vials of various oils. "We tend to go back to our roots in times like this. Each of these items serves a special purpose."

Dylan and Charlie drifted out of the kitchen and back to the den, where the gleeful squeals of cartoon characters echoed from the television.

Lexi stepped forward and threw her arm around Stevie's shoulder. "I'm going to take off now. You'll call if you need anything?"

Stevie gave a slight nod. "Of course."

"You're a terrible liar." Lexi patted her back before she left.

"Oh, how thoughtful." Alice cooed as she held up a small mesh bag filled with dried purple buds. "This is lavender. It's an effective antidepressant. It can also be used as a mild sedative."

With the flick of Stevie's wrist, the refrigerator door swung open. A bottle of wine rose from a shelf and floated toward her. She grabbed it and poured the last of its contents into her glass.

"I already have that covered." She took a sip.

Alice picked through the collection of gifts. "Lavender won't give you a hangover." She pulled a hefty chunk of amber from the bottom of the basket and placed it on the table in front of Stevie. "You already know about this one. It's for strength and protection."

Stevie shook her head and raised her glass to her lips, casting a wary glance toward the golden hued resin. "An entire coven of powerful witches couldn't bring down Susan. What, exactly, do you think that rock is going to do to stop her?"

Alice drew in a deep breath. "I've always thought that we'd gotten lazy over the centuries. We stepped away from our old ways. Now we can blow up boats with our thoughts and refill our glasses without moving from our seats. Believe it or not, there was a time when our magic relied entirely on natural elements." She unloaded the last of the items from the basket, pausing to take in the scent of a handmade candle. "Mmm, hyacinth." She placed it on the table and lit its wick with nothing more than a good, long stare. "Hyacinth is used for overcoming grief."

Stevie picked up a sachet of pungent herbs and rolled it over in her hand. The dried leaves inside crunched in protest as she manhandled them. She knew so little of her people's history, especially with regard to natural magic.

"I have no business leading these witches, Alice." Stevie placed the sachet on the table.

"Of course you do!" Alice's eyes grew wide and her eyebrows shot up. "They need you, Stevie. We need you. I can help you learn everything you need to know."

"If I take on this role as *queen*..." The weight of the word hung in the air between them. "Susan will kill me. Then what will you do?"

Alice's wrinkled hand trembled as she reached for the basket's handle. "You *are* our queen now, Stevie. I know this as sure as I'm standing here. Susan can never hold that honor."

Unconvinced, Stevie dropped her gaze.

"It's ultimately your choice." Alice lifted the empty basket from the table and turned to leave. As she reached the doorway, she spun around to face Stevie once again. "But I believe in you."

Chapter forty-nine

Stevie

Half the town attended Patricia's funeral on Thursday afternoon. The mayor and his wife, along with the town commissioners and their spouses, were all present. Dozens of other families came to pay their respects as well. Many, Stevie knew, were mourning the loss of their secret queen. Others had come to acknowledge the passing of the President of the Historic Society. The shock of her sudden death reverberated in their mournful silence.

Stevie's hair flitted in the cool breeze that blew across the crowded cemetery. Standing between her father and Sam, with Charlie by her side, she listened to the minister speak of Patricia as if he'd known her well. He offered the grieving family solace through the promise of heaven.

Without looking, she knew her loyal coven stood just behind her, ready to offer support as needed. Tucked in amid grieving family members, dignitaries, neighbors, and friends, they were the only mourners who knew the true cause of Patricia's death—a secret they could never divulge.

Stevie tucked a stray hair behind her ear. The time would soon come when she'd have to figure out how to proceed against Susan, but today she would honor Patricia, who had tirelessly served her community, her people, and her family. While everyone else mourned the loss of a venerable woman, she wept for her mentor, her queen, and her mother.

The minister's kind words fell away as background noise as Stevie's mind drifted once again to thoughts of leaving Beaufort. It was what Patricia had wanted. But things were different now. She pressed her hand against her aching heart, wishing she could ask for her mother's advice just one more time.

Stevie stared at the casket that held the body of the woman who had died trying to protect her people. A lover of peace and yet a warrior at heart, her mother had been far more complex than she'd ever imagined. She'd only just begun to know the real Patricia, who had been far more extraordinary than the façade she presented to the world.

The minister led the group in a final prayer.

She bowed her head, struggling to find a middle ground in the dichotomy of her new role. She was woefully underqualified to lead her coven in battle against the darkness that had settled in their town. Yet, her instincts commanded her to rule these people with the same honor and integrity demonstrated by all the queens who had come before her.

Just like her mother had.

Stevie's dad grabbed her hand and gave it a gentle tug. The service had ended.

The crowd began to break up. Stevie stepped forward and placed her hand on the casket. "Goodbye, Mom." She squeezed her eyes shut in a desperate attempt to stop herself from sobbing.

"Stephanie." Jim rested his hand on her back. "Are you okay?"

She blinked to clear her eyes and turned to face him. "Yeah, Dad. I'm fine."

"Let's invite everyone back to the house." He forced a brave smile. "I have five hams and probably close to thirty casseroles. I don't even know how many cakes there are. They keep bringing food…so much food. I'm going to need some help with all of it." His smile faltered as his lip began to tremble. "I'm just going to need some help, honey." He dropped his gaze to the ground and took a ragged breath.

"I know, Dad." She wrapped her arms around her father. "I'm here."

"Miss Stevie?"

Stevie pulled away from her father to see a young girl scampering in her direction. She couldn't have been more than six years old. She wore her hair in curly pigtails secured with blue ribbons. Her mother followed close behind, rushing to keep up with her.

A broad grin stretched across the girl's face as she reached Stevie. Her eyes were bright with excitement. Stevie didn't know her name, but she recognized the girl from Charlie's kindergarten class.

"Miss Stevie, my mom says that you're our new queen. Is that true?"

The little girl's mother cleared her throat and cast a nervous glance in Jim's direction. "She means *president*. President of the Historic Society. Right, sweetie?"

The girl's eyes grew wide, and she blushed at her mistake. She gave a quick nod and looked at Stevie, hopeful.

Stevie's gaze drifted to her mother's casket. She thought of Patricia's strength and her determination. She thought of the young girl who stood before her now and considered what her young life would be like under Susan's reign as queen.

In that moment, she made her decision.

Stevie knelt down, placing herself at eye level with the child. She couldn't help but smile because she knew the answer to the little girl's question with absolute certainty.

"Yes, I am."

About the Author

Chrissy Lessey is a beach bum with a deep appreciation for good jokes, strong coffee, and salt air. She lives on the beautiful Crystal Coast of North Carolina where she finds endless opportunities to procrastinate and daydream. A long-time fan of rock music, Chrissy married a talented drummer. She still loves listening to him play—as long as it's not in the house. Together, they have two energetic children and an ill-mannered dog.

She enjoys connecting with her fans both in person and online. Visit ChrissyLessey.com or follow her on Facebook, Twitter, and Instagram to stay up-to-date on her latest book news and upcoming appearances.

praise for the crystal coast series

"*The Coven* is atmospheric, intriguing, and at times deeply moving. With terrific characters, a vivid setting, and plot that clips along smartly, this book is a great read. A series to dive into!"

-Paula Brackston,
New York Times Bestselling Author of *The Witch's Daughter*

"Very well-written, easy to read and engaging. I was surprised by how much I cared about the characters. For me, this demonstrates Lessey's ability to cross genre boundaries and engage ALL readers."

-Steph Post,
author of *Lightwood*

"Lessey's story is both heartwarming and surprisingly believable."

-C.H. Armstrong,
author of *The Edge of Nowhere*

"I devoured this book in one sitting! *The Coven* opens the reader's mind to the magic all around us. Ms. Lessey's beautiful account of the lengths a mother will go to for her child is splattered with a family's age-old quest for revenge, a touch of romance, and a loving account of a small town community's bond and commitment to each other. Fans of Nora Roberts' light paranormal stories (Cousins O'Dwyer Trilogy, Three Sisters Island Trilogy) will love *The Coven*."

-Jessica Calla,
author of The Sheridan Hall Series and *The Love Square*

"It's *Practical Magic* meets *Steel Magnolias*."

-Chanda Platania,
Neuse Regional Library

"Chrissy Lessey doesn't disappoint with her fast-paced, easy-to-read, enjoyable witch story. I loved the setting and the relationship between Stevie and her son Charlie, who has autism. The connection of the witches to the famous pirate Blackbeard is a great twist."

-Teri Harman,
author of The Moonlight Trilogy

"*The Coven* is extraordinary for two reasons. First, it is a well-written story with fully developed characters. The story draws you in and doesn't let go. The second reason I love *The Coven* is the way the author treats her autistic character. Too often, these depictions wind up being caricatures of autism. Chrissy Lessey manages to avoid this by presenting a realistic character who is multifaceted and engaging. My heartfelt thanks for that."

-Josh Leone,
author of The Calling Tower Saga